LOST IN INFINITY

Travis Besecker (signature)

TRAVIS BESECKER

PROLOGUE

The rain tickled my window with a lullaby of sand and tin as the darkness that engulfed the house crept down the hallway and invaded my room. The light from the street lamp shining through my bedroom window was momentarily enraged, flooding the room in a bright explosion of white. My pupils narrowed, leaving the room black once again. Slowly the street lamp beyond began to return to its full luminosity as the hint of a rumble erupted overhead. The thunder built to a crescendo, rolling over the house with such force that my window rattled in its frame. The street lamp, irritated by the flash of light, slowly acclimated back to the dark of night, returning the spilled light to the back wall of my room before the next flash of lightning was able to recycle the process all over again.

My pupils dilated and the shadow behind my dresser came

into focus once again. My soccer trophy stretched out along the wood paneling turning a plated plastic bicycle kick into an elongated triceratops holding a zeppelin. I focused my thoughts on the shadow, imagining why a dinosaur would ever need an airship, when the shadow shifted. The triceratops turned its head to look at me. I looked back at the trophy confused and the shadow turned away. My gaze returned to the zeppelin and another shadow grew in the corner near my closet door. I looked directly at the shadow. It looked back. Another flash of lightning and my room was reset.

The shadow returned with the onslaught of my focus. This time, as I stared at the shadow, a face appeared in my doorway, sneaking around the corner of the dark oak frame. I sat up in bed and whipped my head in its direction. Gone. Out of the corner of my peripheral vision appeared another face. I turned my head slowly and it disappeared just the same. The faces would never allow me to see them directly. They were always there and always gone. The shadow creatures watched from just beyond the attention of my eyes. They would hide within the darkness, out of sight but close enough they were not afraid to be seen. Another flash of lightning and my room was reset.

The looming face in the corner stared back at me through black eyes. I ignored the shy faces watching and waiting behind furniture and around corners so that I could peer into the deep black that was The Shadow Man. He blinked and the black was gone. Sheer terror washed over me as the movement took root in my brain. A scream escaped my lungs and pierced the 3am silence. Until this moment my mind was so lost in curiosity that I had rationalized the faces and The Shadow Man as tricks of light. They were more interesting than frightening. Interesting shadows did not blink…

What is deja vu? In French it literally means, "already seen". Emile Boirac, a French psychic researcher, coined the term. Déjà vu is the feeling that one has already seen or experienced the current situation before, even though the circumstances may be vague, unclear or uncertain. It's the feeling of "I've been here and done this before." The feeling can accompany something as simple as watching a car pass or bending over to pick up a piece of paper. It can be as unnerving as knowing every word of a conversation before it is spoken… or at least feeling as if you do. The most frequent explanation is that the experience *did* happen before. Picking up a piece of paper seems so random that believing it has happened before may be a simple coincidence. Another plausible explanation is that the feeling is caused by a breakdown in the neurological system. Imagine the systems responsible for short and long term memory misfiring or firing nanoseconds apart. The result is a memory planted in the psyche before the conscious part of the brain ever receives the information and processes it, giving the illusion of past experience.

I've felt deja vu on a daily basis since I was a child. Whether I'm brushing my teeth or looking down and noticing the cracks in the sidewalk passing by underfoot, as soon as the feeling overcomes me, my heart starts to race. At first I found it exciting. I wondered if there was some hidden talent that I possessed but was yet unable to hone... Or maybe it was hereditary. One day a great grandparent would approach me with the inevitable speech about great responsibility and our secret Native American ancestry... My brain always finds the most outlandish and impossible explanations. It's in my nature. I've always had a wild imagination.

Precognition may not be a viable theory, but it was for a long time the most entertaining. Whenever the feeling of deja vu struck me, I would imagine the moment in time as a request for assistance by the forces of fate. My brain was being triggered for a greater good, making me notice something small in that instance and giving me the opportunity to change my path or make a difference in the lives of the less fortunate. I'd roll the dice and turn up four sixes and a two in the middle of a game of Yahtzee and get the feeling of deja vu... instead of re-rolling the two and going for a signature "Yahtzee!", I'd scoop up the sixes and re-roll the four-of-a-kind for more twos. I'd smile and block out the catcalls from my competitors letting me know how stupid I was because deep down inside I knew that with that shake and toss of those four dice, came a change in our timeline and the path of the world around me. I was saving a life or righting a wrong.

Chaos theory and the Butterfly effect became obsessions as a result of my fascination with déjà vu. I began to wonder what good I was doing by each and every action. I began to worry what wrong I was causing with them as well. The worry started to affect my ability to make quick and intelligent decisions. Double and triple guessing each action and choice to see if a double negative would somehow correct the possibility of a mudslide in Rio de Janeiro or a piano falling on a woman pushing her baby in a buggy in Paris...

Time travel fascinated me. From H.G. Wells to Carl Sagan, I wanted to know everything about it. Wormholes, black holes, Einstein's Theory of Relativity, the space-time continuum... I ventured into every aspect of its possibilities. I even went as far as creating markers in time for future time travelers to be able to use as calibration points for their eventual time traveling devices. I waited and wondered. I knew that one day, when I stood in the street looking up at the sky with my sign clearly marking the time and date down to the second that a traveler from the future would magically appear before me with a thank you and a pat on the head. When that moment never arrived, I began to speculate about what that meant. Time was a construct created as a crutch to put boundaries on the things our young minds were unable to comprehend. Time was irrelevant. If time was irrelevant, what else had no point or meaning? Religion? Life? Death? Why are we here? Where is here? What is the meaning of life?

All before I was seven.

This is just a glimpse at how my mind works.

I stop, I think, I worry. Repeat.

If I'm not worrying about decisions or consequences, I'm questioning the validity of the actions and reactions. Accepting the truths of others leaves no room for the possibility of enlightenment that comes from an answer for which the question was never asked. I ask a lot of questions. It's my nature. I've always had a wild imagination.

What is déjà vu? What does it mean to you? By the time you finish this book, your answer may change.

"Why are you here?" I whispered.

The Shadow Man blinked and goose bumps ran from my wrists to my spine. I pulled the covers tighter and sunk deeper into my pillow. Silence filled my room then gave way to my labored breathing followed by the shock of another distant roll of thunder.

Enjoy the show.

PART I

INTRODUCTIONS

CHAPTER 1

MY CONFESSION

Hi, my name is Travis. I'm an insomniac with apeirophobia. I am many things. I am a father, a lover, a designer and a comedian.

I am not a writer.

I figure that's as good a place as any to start. I hope that once you begin reading this book, you'll discover it's much more than the story of my life and times. Living with insomnia and apeirophobia has been an internal struggle between repressed fear and straightforward optimism. I've never before been able to open up publicly about my inner struggles, however, over the last year, I've found a way to work through them by sharing the burden. I'm optimistic that through the completion of this work, I'll be able to sleep at night knowing someone (anyone) knows the secrets I've harbored for more than I'm able to remember or know.

I have a confession to make. Everything I've done in my life has been leading up to the following summation of events. One of you is going to read this and it will redefine everything you thought you knew about yourself, about life, about existence... about *everything*. If you're not the person this book is intended for, you can either stop now or read on and enjoy the show.

There is a memory locked deep in my subconscious that's been sitting dormant since I was a child. With the help of The Shadow Man and my own inner voice, the memory has been fighting to reach the surface. For decades I have misconstrued the suppression as just another exaggerated conspiracy created in the wake of my insomnia and apeirophobia, but as the mysteries of my past unravel so do the answers to the questions that have plagued me across time and space.

When I was a kid, the fear of infinity and the vast nothingness of our existence within the universe drove my parents to send me to countless psychiatrists. All attempted the same thing, but none were able to give me anything more than tools to better accomplish suppressing the fear rather than facing it.

One of the psychiatrists I confided in, after feeling our sessions had run their course, asked me to meet with a new colleague. I agreed without hesitation. Either because I was a kid and didn't know any better or I was desperate for help, I do not know. I started to see this new psychiatrist exclusively after my parents were approached with an offer to treat me pro bono. I would receive a place in their new test group in turn for their signed approval to use me as part of an upcoming Medical Journal case study.

As you begin to read this book, you will undoubtedly ask, "Is this fiction?" The tale I'm about to tell you is the story of my life. It contains truths, dreams, recollections and suppressed memories. Whether or not it is fact or fiction is irrelevant. What is the difference really? Do you truly know that the life you are experiencing is real? What convinces you that the world your body is floating through is anything more than the culmination of billions and billions of synapses firing across your brain telling you that you are doing the things you are doing? How naïve is it to accept this as fact when the only truth you can be completely sure of is that the synapses *are* firing, relaying the message. Beyond the message, nothing else is guaranteed. You accept the rest on faith. It's a paradigm that surpasses question. I question everything. It's in my nature. I have a wild imagination.

The story I'm about to tell you is the untold chapters of my life, finally laid out in one comprehensive collection ultimately unveiling the truth behind every lie I've been trapped within for as long as I can remember. This book is a means to an end for me. I have to get this off of my chest. No matter the consequences. No matter the aftermath. This must be done.

One of you is going to read this. You may have already read it a thousand times before. One of you is going to read this and it will change the course of your life. It will perpetuate the course of your life. It will perpetuate the course of time. This book was meant for you.

Forgive me.

CHAPTER 2

INSOMNIA

The smell of lilacs was so potent it bordered on toxic. I was forced to take a breath, hold it and then release through pursed lips. A candle store going up in flames would have been easier to stomach than this waiting room. My eyes started to water, which could be misconstrued as tears, pissing me off instantly. Stupid flowers. I swung my legs freely in the solitary chair while my hands tapped out a beat on the dark stained oak armrests. The window to my left was covered in matching dark wood blinds, turned slightly toward the ceiling. A broken rainbow of sunlight peeked

through and danced on the contrasting hardwood
floor as clouds slowly made their way beyond the
confines of my holding cell...

In today's day and age, everybody claims to be an insomniac. That word gets thrown around an awful lot. It's popular, it's hip and it's accepted. The problem is 99% of the people who claim to be insomniacs are people with poor sleep routines, drug addictions or the inability to tell the truth. Staying up late at night does not constitute insomnia. Being so tired you fall asleep standing at a checkout with a bottle of Diet Mountain Dew in your hand and a MasterCard halfway through the card reader because you haven't been able to sleep longer than twenty minutes in six days, *does*.

There are three types of insomnia. The first is Transient, which usually lasts a few days and is most commonly caused by stress. The second is Acute, which can last up to a month and be caused by a variety of factors from stress to medication non-compliance. The last type of insomnia is the mother of all sleeplessness, Chronic Insomnia.

Chronic Insomnia can last years, even decades. Most often Chronic Insomnia is caused by another disorder or mental illness. The symptoms can include muscle fatigue, double vision, hallucinations and major medical complications. Many chronic insomniacs experience blackouts or micronaps where they more or less sleep walk through their day. They function near normally but can't recall a single event when asked afterward. Have you ever driven to work and forgotten the journey once you pulled into the parking lot? This was likely because the drive to work has become routine and your mind memorizes the motions. Your body ran on autopilot. What about waking up in the morning and not being able to recall when or how you made it to bed? Imagine if you went through your entire day, then got into bed feeling the same way, unable to remember how you got there.

I, unfortunately, was diagnosed with Chronic Insomnia at age seven. I'm now thirty-five. For nearly three decades I've experienced sleepless nights, micronaps, blackouts, hallucinations, fear and confusion. The insomnia comes and goes with extreme fluctuations. I can spend a month getting less than two hours of sleep each day, often broken down into twenty-minute naps. Then my body finally takes over and crashes. A mental reboot; my brain flips from flight to fight and assumes control before systems start to shut down from fatigue. I will finally fall asleep and can be dead to the world for up to twenty hours straight. Other times my body can survive off of three to four hours a night for months on end before finally crashing. Then, in the most extreme cases, usually brought on debilitating stress, I have been known to stay awake for upward of seventy hours before napping only to do it again and again. These instances are followed by epic down times. A weekend in bed disguised by a mask of flu accompanied by stomachaches, vomiting and the desire to die become my mental crash of choice.

My insomnia is both a curse and a savior. I'm also a workaholic with an active imagination and a mind that never slows or stops. I'm not happy unless I have countless irons in the fire. My insomnia allows me to stay active in a variety of projects and fields. The more things I have going on, the easier it is to stay focused on the task at hand rather than letting my mind wonder into deeper darker territory. Sleeping is, and always has been, the enemy. When I finally do find my way to the realm of unconscious travel, the moment of return is ripe with regret. Every minute spent asleep is a minute lost, never to return.

When I was young and the insomnia was first introduced into my life, I didn't know how to handle the experience. At first, the sleepless nights were caused by my brain's inability to rest or turn off. I would lie in bed at night, stare at my ceiling and contemplate my own existence until the sun came up. As one night turned into two, turned into three, I started to see things... scary things. Things like reflections in my bedroom window, faces in the shadows and even things running by my bedroom door in the darkness of the living room beyond. Being seven years old, I did nothing short of freak out. Unfortunately, these hallucinations grew darker and more alive as the condition progressed.

My parents had just given birth to my baby sister so explaining to them what was going on prompted immediate dismissal. It was assumed I was simply looking for some attention in a house newly focused on the arrival of a second child. After a few days of no sleep during the night, I started falling asleep during the day at inopportune times. My parents received a phone call from the nurse at my school asking for a conference. By Friday, I was at my family physician.

My pediatrician felt the same as my parents, discarding my new sleep routine as a reaction to no longer being the center of attention. A week turned into a month and my routine did not change. As long as I was occupied with something, I was fine. As a mediocre attempt to pass the time, I would watch television until the American Flag test pattern appeared and then read until morning. My parents assumed it would pass, but as it progressed and did not, I found the end of their leniency.

My parents resorted to punishment for my nighttime behavior. I assume that some of you are going to see this as me immediately painting them as the bad guys. I assure you, this is not the case. I don't want you to hold this against them. I've often wondered how I would have handled it as a parent myself. They labeled it behavioral based on my doctor's recommendation. They forbid me from leaving my room at night so the television became off limits. In turn, I resorted to reading. Next they removed my lamp - I found a flashlight. They took the flashlight – I started frequenting the bathroom. And so on. By the end I was left with only the dark and my imagination to drive me to the edge of sanity on the back of a horse named Sleep Deprivation.

Instead of giving up, I fought harder. I wanted to sleep. I wanted it so badly I decided to exhaust myself with activity. I was already a seven year old so being active was second nature, but normal adolescent activity would not suffice. I needed exhaustion to force my body into submission. I'd bought an Atari 2600 that summer with birthday money, allowance and pinched pennies for $49.95 at Sears. I'd also earned enough to pick up a used black and white 13" television at a garage sale. This was my first major purchase and something I'd worked long and hard to achieve so when I asked my dad to disconnect it, he agreed but sat me down to discuss why.

I explained to my parents that I was going to try to exhaust myself every day, outside, in the heat, in an effort to make falling asleep at night a necessity. The Atari was a distraction and needed to go. It was at this point that my parents decided maybe I wasn't just seeking attention. Their anger finally turned to sympathy.

At night, without the television or light to read by, I resorted to my imagination. I would close my eyes tight to avoid the shadows and faces that my mind would convince me were watching the melodrama of my mental collapse. Instead of contemplating existence, I decided to build a place in my head that I could go to every night. The dream world in my brain consisted of a quarantined town, encased in a glass dome, where only I remained. I could go anywhere and do whatever I wanted without consequence. Some nights I'd break into the mall and play video games to my heart's content. Other nights I'd steal cars or even burn buildings to the ground. I could live out my wildest fantasies in this mythical town while no one was the wiser. It kept my mind occupied and my nights busy in the confines of my darkened bedroom. I was well protected from the frightening darkness, hiding in the solitude of my own mind.

Still, the sleepless nights continued without reprieve. Nearly half a year passed before my father asked me to come to the living room for a family discussion. When I arrived my mother was already crying and my dad looked concerned.

"What's wrong?" I asked.

"Your mother and I want to know what you need to help fix this." My dad would only look at my mom or his hands… never into my eyes. Giving me the impression that this was not his doing, but hers.

"Fix what?" I asked.

"You're not sleeping, honey. We're concerned." My mother rose and walked slowly to where I stood. Before she reached me with her outstretched hand, I sat down in the chair, looking at her bell collection in the curio cabinet rather than either of them.

"Why now?" I asked. For months I had been put off, brushed aside and discounted as a jealous sibling. Their change of heart was too little, too late at this point. I wasn't relieved. I was pissed. They had been part of the problem, not the solution.

"Your mother thinks this situation is growing dire." My dad stood and grabbed my mom's hand to stop her from approaching me. "I am standing firm here. This isn't helping. This is going to make it worse." The last was directed at her. I could only tell by the change in inflection because my eyes never left the porcelain angel bell with arms stretched skyward looking up at the glass shelf overhead. All I could imagine is the tiny blue angel looking under the ceramic dress of the Scarlet O'Hare bell located directly above.

"Then leave me be. I'm his mother and I'm going to do what I think's best." My mother stepped away from my father and took a seat on the armrest of my chair. "Travis, dear, what can I do to help?"

My father stood for a moment; arms crossed and watched the scene unfold. I didn't say a word. The bell next to Scarlet was a reflective silver miniature Liberty Bell, complete with a crack. Collecting bells seemed so pointless. Why bells? I remained silent.

"Travis, we'll do whatever you want." My mother offered, which was immediately followed with a huff from my father. I looked up in just enough time to see him exit the living room for the kitchen and a bowl of cereal.

"I want to be able to sleep. You can't fix that." I exited victorious to the soundtrack of Cheerios being poured. The nerve of my parents.

At the time, this conversation completely pissed me off. I remember going to my room and wishing I'd never be able to sleep again. I didn't want to fall asleep any time soon just in case they thought the conversation I'd just been ambushed with had any part in the recovery. This was my problem. I was going to solve it.

I didn't solve it. The problem persisted. To make things even worse, about a month after the first "family conversation", my father approached me for a second one. Looking back on it now, I think it was genuine concern. Twenty-eight years ago, I blew it off as him trying to satisfy my mother. He offered to do whatever it took to make me sleep again. I was promised a color television for my room, a new bike and a vacation with my grandparents to see relatives in Oklahoma. It was even put on the table that my parents were willing to paint my bedroom black because it was something I'd joked about before my sister was born. This was suggested after I'd spent months petrified of faces in my shadows and figures moving around my room in my sleep deprived hallucination driven bedtime ritual. I refused it all.

My parents were clueless to my problem and the true cause. It was impossible to explain then, as a seven year old. It's no less confusing attempting to put it into words now, almost three decades later.

CHAPTER 3

APEIROPHOBIA

I looked up at the receptionist, Christie, busy typing away loudly behind the raised counter. The whir and hum of the electric typewriter competed with the soft woodwinds floating down out of the ceiling tile speakers. Her typing echoed through the office, breaking the monotony with each fevered stroke. I counted the key clicks and tried to imagine the words as they inked the page. In my head she was writing a letter to the editor of the daily newspaper about how furious she was with the current state of affairs surrounding the shade of red illuminating from the city's stoplights.

The red light, according to a study she'd read in a medical journal, actually incited violence toward women. She was requesting the stoplights be changed to blue/yellow/white instead of red/yellow/green in order to cut down on the ever-growing problem of domestic abuse. Christie looked up and smiled. I looked down and blushed...

I live a double life.

I have an irrational fear of the universe as an infinite space. I suffer from Apeirophobia. I know it's an irrational fear; it's a stupid thing to get hung up on. I realize me worrying about it is pointless, but that doesn't make it any less real... only more annoying.

Apeirophobia is a generalized phobia for a multitude of fears that are often so unexplainable they get lumped under one title. It manifests itself in many different ways. It's, for sake of argument, the fear of infinity. Some psychiatrists diagnose Apeirophobia as the fear of immortal life. That's not my version of the fear. Immortality would be awesome. I'd finally get my to-do list finished.

My Apeirophobia is much harder to explain. The distance

between my bed and the wall does not freak me out in the middle of the night. Some apeirophobics can't handle the concept of repeating number sequences. The number π doesn't bother me. I assume there is a pattern to the chaos, the problem is we are too naïve in our intellect to comprehend or see it. My Apeirophobia centers on the known and unknown universe. My fear is the fear of infinite expansion. I can't stare into the star filled night sky without having some kind of panic attack. The concept of the never-ending nothingness comprising deep space makes my brain lock up like a Ford Pinto fitted with a busted oil pan. The concept of space and the reality that makes up our entire existence, without beginning or end, what it is, where it is and *when* it is... makes my brain shut out everything but the circle of thought leading me back and forth from my own consciousness, to thought, to life, to existence, to space, to the beginning of time, to the end of time and back again... Then, somewhere in the mix, I start to count... counting calms me. I count everything. How many steps to the restroom? How many stairs to the second floor? How many seconds does the traffic light average? How many prime numbers do I know without math? Fibonacci, Descartes, Nietzsche, Archimedes, 2, 3, 5, 7, 11, 13, 17, 19, 23... ugh. Breathe. *Just breathe damnit.*

Imagine, every time you saw an egg, your brain would drown everything else out and think about nothing but what came first... the chicken or the egg? That's it. Just that. Nothing else. Chicken? Egg? Chicken? Egg? Can't sleep. Chicken? Egg? Can't function. Chicken? Egg?

That's my Apeirophobia in a nutshell.

I first developed the fear in Sunday School. I was five years old and enrolled in Bible study because my mother couldn't satisfy my constant questions about God. Remember, I ask a lot of questions. She turned to her pastor who suggested the lessons learned in Sunday School would squelch my misgivings about religion. During the first week, my mom was asked to keep me home. I was not welcome to return because my skepticism was distracting the other children. My mother has all but blocked this out of her memory because it "was one of the most embarrassing moments" of her adult life. My constant questions about existence coupled with my disbelief in everything unable to be proven with anything more than smoke and mirrors prompted deep seeded frustration and eventually led me down the lonely path to Atheism. This was my first experience with the concept of infinite expansion. I could not bring myself to believe that space ended in "heaven".

A few years later when I was about seven, while watching "You Only Live Twice", the James Bond film, my Apeirophobia went into overdrive and prompted my before mentioned, and currently continued, bouts with insomnia. Beyond the sleepless nights, the fear brought along with it several lovely facial ticks. After a few years of therapy, the fear finally subsided to where I could function but never fully went away. The facial ticks and twitches come back with stress. I also get recurring lockjaw as well as ulcers when the tension levels rise too high. As long as I can maintain an even keel I'm good to go, but once things get out of hand, it all comes crashing back like I got hit in the face with the asylum stick.

For the last twenty-five years, I've pretended it doesn't bother me. I've tried to face it head on, but when it's the fear of infinity, how the fuck do you face it? You don't. What *I* have done is perfected the art of forced sleep, catnaps and pretending to snore, doze and nod off.

In all honesty, it's not *always* fake. At times, exhaustion takes the wheel and my body just shuts down. If it's bad enough, I can appear near narcoleptic. These instances come a few times each month when the micronapping starts. I'll begin with sleep walking during the day. Before long, I'm sending notes and emails, having full on incoherent conversations with family, friends and co-workers… all during a state of semi-consciousness. I've been told it's entertaining, funny and sometimes kind of frightening. I also get belligerent when this stage kicks in. I get irritated and pissed that sleep's coming, fighting the urge like a toddler kicking and screaming… Then I finally lose the last few hours of consciousness in a haze of regret and apology.

Sleep finally hits me like a brick wall. My brain flips from fight to flight and assumes control before systems start to shut down from fatigue. I will finally fall asleep and can be dead to the world for up to twenty hours straight. Afterward, it's like waking up from a dream and having just the hint of remembering you had one. You know you experienced something, but the details are still foggy. The worst part is the post sleep shutdown. My body feels like I'm coming off of pneumonia or stuck with the 24-hour flu.

I live a double life. Twenty-five years of this and I'm only just now starting to talk about it. A few people "know" about it, but that's only because they've witnessed it or been privy to it firsthand. Everyone else just thinks, "Man, he's a night owl" or "How does he run on a couple hours of sleep?" They don't know that I've wrecked my car nine times over the years from falling asleep at the wheel. They don't know that I've had to take time off of work and school for embarrassing ticks, twitches and an inability to eat or talk from TMJ. They don't know that when I close my eyes, if I'm not already deep in thought about something else, I instantly think about vast nothingness.

Some apeirophobics fear space... not only outer space, but also personal space. They must be in contact with something at all times. Other apeirophobics fear life without end or life without the existence of a supreme power. A few apeirophobics even fear π and the concept of a number so large it has no end...

I fear the infinite expansion of time and space. I fear reality without beginning or end. I worry about the confines of the universe. Where is it? What is it? Where does it begin? Where does it end? I worry about the confines of time. When is it? How did it begin? How can it end? Why are we here? What is the meaning of life?

Who am I? Why am I? When am I? These are the questions that keep my brain twisting and turning.

There is but only one truth. *I am me.* I think, therefore I am.

*It was **the egg** and not the egg, by the way. The chicken's DNA was already in the egg when it was created to encapsulate the first mutated chicken zygote.*

CHAPTER 4

STRESS

This wasn't the first office I'd been to and I doubted it would be the last. Recently, my parents had decided to the fact that their son did not think the way other people think. My pediatrician had pointed out that my problems were not being corrected by conventional means; it was time to move on to a more unconventional approach. Against everything they'd ever told themselves, I was turned over to the educated assistance of a therapist. I was actively a member of the community of lost souls, spilling their darkest innermost thoughts to a trained professional. Soon

I'd be asked, "How does that make you feel?" and prompted "let's explore this deeper," while I basically worked through my own issues. The psychiatrist was nothing more than a mediator between my body and my mind. Once again, someone else would be taking credit for me solving my own problems...

Speaking of the chicken and the egg, one of the biggest factors related to my apeirophobia and, subsequently, my insomnia, is stress. The apeirophobia causes insomnia. The insomnia causes stress. Stress makes the apeirophobia worse, making the insomnia worse, giving me more stress... Once I'm stuck in this vicious circle, it can quickly spiral out of control.

The stress brings with it an entourage of insidious cohorts. Not only does it affect my sleep patterns, it causes twitches, ticks, lockjaw, digestive issues and a depleted immune system, which usually ends with me out of commission suffering from the current illness of choice. If I'm lucky, whatever is ailing me will eventually prompt a physical collapse, breaking the cycle and ultimately creating a large enough lull to get me back on track.

I developed my first tick at age seven as part of my initial introduction to insomnia. It came in the form of my right eyelid twitching and my right upper cheek contracting. I was cursed with a perpetual wink. It sounds funny now but for a self-conscious second grader it was horrible. I quickly learned the art of brooding off into the distance to look both interesting and deep in thought while, in reality, hiding my twitches by turning my head away from my conversational partner. The twitch lasted a few months before it was sporadic and finally non-existent. The return to normal was not due to my own volition. I'd have to thank my family doctor and a cocktail of meds prescribed to relax and subdue a prepubescent adolescent with an over active imagination and a penchant for self destruction. The twitch comes and goes to this day. Sunglasses and a quick wit can usually combat most ridicule but sleep and relaxation work just as well.

About ten years ago, I woke up one morning and found it difficult to brush my teeth. I didn't think anything of it and actually chose to blame the issue on my new toothbrush. By lunch, I noticed I could only open my mouth wide enough to fit a ballpoint pen between my teeth. Eating was rendered impossible unless I wanted to go on a liquid diet or eat baby food through a straw. I was on antibiotics at the time for a chest cold so I ignored the lockjaw, assuming the meds would take care of it on their own. By the weekend, the problem had corrected itself and I assumed some sort of hidden infection was to blame. A few years passed and once again I found myself eating pancakes and drinking through a straw. Again, it passed. A few years after, it returned. This time, with a vengeance. I was unable to eat or drink because the second morning arrived with a jaw unable to separate my teeth. The next day I was sitting in the chair at my dentist's office while he checked for an abscessed tooth and prepped me for an x-ray. The results confirmed; my only course of action was to relieve the stress. I was fitted for a night guard to help cut down on my teeth grinding and given a hall pass for a bottle of anti-depressants to help cut down on my teeth clamping. I refused to fill the prescription or buy the mouth guard, instead opting for "Option B" which consisted of Guinness through a straw, a collection of horror movies and a weekend trip to Tennessee with friends.

I am a workaholic. When you have this many irons in fire, it's impossible to end the day burn free. I finish everything I start too. One of the upsides to insomnia is a 22 hour workday if need be. The stress can be most effectively trumped by finishing projects and moving forward. I'm on so many committees, boards and volunteer groups that even when the workday ends, I'm faced with a dozen other obligations. I'm also a licensed soccer coach, a conditioning director and a contributor for half a dozen websites. Did I mention a second job, five blogs and Webmaster for eleven websites totaling a million-plus new visitors monthly? I bring it all on myself so I'm not looking for pity, I'm simply explaining that there is little or no time left for "me".... for "my life". This creates even more stress. The older I get and the more complicated my world becomes, the less time I have to reduce the stress constructively.

As an unwritten rule, every one of my personal outlets eventually becomes a responsibility. I have an overly obsessive personality (common with apeirophobia) so I immediately strip the joy out of even the most trivial activities. For example, I used to have time to play video games. Each time I did, it became something else to obsess over. I would research all known variations, strategies and outcomes. I'd spend hours making spreadsheets detailing every aspect, medal, achievement, trophy, board, character, map, weapon, etc. Then, when it became possible to build yourself into the game as a 3-dimensional avatar, I'd spend weeks perfecting my character to a near exact digital replica of my likeness. I've even created digital texture maps of my tattoos pixel by pixel because I found it impossible to enjoy 18 holes of golf on a virtual TPC Sawgrass with a modeled rendering of myself that wasn't as lifelike as possible.

Besides video games, I've taken up several hobbies over the years in an attempt to take my mind off of my struggles with existence, all of which have become new and interesting additions to my daily routine, none of which were effective as stress relievers. Did I mention my inability to quit anything? Once I start something, I am wired to refuse any type of failure, even by way of quitting something that no longer gives me joy. I've learned to refrain from collecting anything because once I begin, I'll break my bank account and obsess over it until I've completed the set or filed bankruptcy. I'm exaggerating of course. I've never really filed bankruptcy. Once again, that'd be admitting failure. I have, however, driven west across two states through the night. Camped in front of a Toys R Us huddled in a lawn chair, wrapped in blankets to keep from getting frostbite. Then spent $5 before turning around and heading home, merely because the die-cast alloy character sitting on the seat beside me was only being released in Chicago, in a select few toy stores, in a package variation that had already shipped before it was caught and corrected.

CHAPTER 5

OBSESSION

"How old are you?" the receptionist asked. I ignored her as long as I could get away with it. It wasn't that I was being rude, it was just that I was trying to avoid the impure thoughts that ran through my head at night thinking back to her smile, her glasses, her ponytail bouncing as she typed away on the humming typewriter deep in her personal memoirs about how she was obsessed with stealing a young boy's virginity and welcoming him to manhood by way of her seductive charm and heavenly perfume... or that's how I'd imagine it later when I told The Shadow

Man about the afternoon's events. Did I mention I was sexually advanced and frustrated as an eight year old? "Oh fine, ignore me. You must be the strong silent type." This time I looked up. Sure enough, Christie peeked over the top of her horn-rimmed glasses with perfect hazel eyes, a smile and a tiny pointed chin propped up on two slender hands. I smiled then remembered she was waiting for an answer so I held up both hands, in an effort to display ten outstretched fingers. Okay, I lied. Not a big lie, but blinded by my hormone riddled adolescence I assumed I had a better shot with her If she at least thought I'd breached into the world of double digits...

Part of the common factors associated with apeirophobia is obsessive-compulsive tendencies. Some sufferers harbor an obsession with germs and compulsive hand washing or fears that a certain routine will result in the irrational death of loved ones. Others have more commonly recognized OCD habits of counting, repetitions of tasks and a failure to move on without completing these tasks. The lucky few have milder compulsions and, in my opinion, are only addressed as such because they also have apeirophobia.

Who doesn't have obsessions of some sort? Even the most normal among us MUST have their doughnut house blend coffee with two squirts of fat free vanilla syrup and four packs of Sweet 'n' Low for breakfast or their day just can't seem to get started. Right? That doesn't mean they have OCD or an obsessive-compulsive tendency. It just means they really fucking love coffee. I really fucking love coffee.

I am one of the lucky ones. I do have obsessive-compulsive traits, but for the most part, I'm highly functional. I like to consider it as a drive for perfection instead of a disorder. I finish what I start. I'm not a quitter. I'm highly devoted. Some people would call it an addiction, others an obsession. I call it love.

"Love" is like wrapping a warm blanket, fresh from the dryer, around your body and snuggling up with a cup of hot cocoa. It makes you feel toasty inside, ready to take on the world. It's infectious; those around you feel the warmth and bask in your dedication. It radiates… brings smiles and giggles of joy. You can't help but ooze happiness.

Alas, "Love" can slowly creep across the threshold into the realm of "Obsession" without you ever knowing it. One day those around you feel your joy and reciprocate it ten-fold, the next they'll blow off your happiness as delirium and throw their pity at you like a public stoning. "He's obsessed, it's so sad" their eyes seem to say. No more the celebration of excitement for your passion. Now, those around you become apathetic to your rants about the compulsion. They no longer care, but as the fixation gets its claws buried deeper, you begin to recede. Who cares? It's mine. My own private escape. That warm blanket and cup of hot cocoa are still wrapped tight, but obsession wraps it tighter and keeps the cups coming. And coming. You can't imagine taking the blanket off or running out of cocoa. In fact, let's mix some Red Bull in with the chocolate so you can stay awake and enjoy more time… in the blanket…

"Obsession" begot "Addiction". Slowly (but surely), the obsession will once again take you further down the spiral. The next thing you know, the blanket is so tight and hot, you're feverish and can barely breathe. The cups of hot cocoa give way to black coffee and cigarettes. There's a voice in your head, contemplating life without the blanket… without the coffee. As certain as the sun will rise and set, so shall you die without your fix. You can't admit it, but no matter what you do to break away, you MUST return. You've reached rock bottom.

There's nowhere to go but up.

It's a good thing too, because at this point you've milked the obsession for all it's worth. The challenge is lost. Boredom creeps in and your life slowly returns to normal. My obsessions come in all forms. Whatever I start, I must finish. I must know every detail in and out. If it's a video game, I need to understand and complete every aspect. I'll make spreadsheets and buy guides. I'll forgo sleep, food and sex to complete the task at hand. The same rules apply to everything else as well. Any type of collection, whether it is toys or books or movies, consumes me. I have to finish. Failure is never an option.

Every day is a struggle. Understanding the obsessions and their place in the realm of my apeirophobia allows me to work through them, but it still doesn't make them take up any less of my time or relieve any more stress. Instead, they become part of the problem.

CHAPTER 6

INTELLIGENCE

She tilted her head and smirked, obviously wooed by my prowess. I mentally patted myself on the back for the last minute decision to bump myself to ten. The more I thought about it, ten is a perfectly acceptable, well-rounded number; a perfect ten, base ten, the metric system, ten fold... I smiled and let it reach all the way to my eyes. When I wanted to, I could be charming as hell. When I needed to, I could be ruthlessly adorable. I had so many women wrapped around my fingers with a flash of deep brown eyes and a toothy smile that I could get away with damn near anything. I winked.

Her smirk relaxed until her jaw dropped between her palms and her eyes showed more white than hazel. Her astonished look confirmed I'd surprised her. My smile grew wider. Her eyes grew to match. "Ten?" she asked. I nodded vigorously. She sat back in her chair and crossed her arms over her chest. Her mouth no longer agape, a thin-lipped smile appeared as she slowly shook her head back and forth. "You're trouble, mister." I continued to nod vigorously...

When I was a toddler, my aunt, who was a kindergarten teacher, urged my mother to bring me to her classroom during enrollment evaluations. Because of my late summer birthday I wasn't scheduled to begin school for two more years. My mom, seeing it as an opportunity to complete some errands, dropped me off and went about her business. Upon returning she was greeted with two things. One, my evaluation, and two, a report that I'd stuck my tongue out at all of the evaluators. She was not happy. I still hear about how embarrassed she was that day. The evaluation? Oh, I passed… exceeded expectations in fact. I was already reading at age three, as well as operating with a full understanding of entry-level first grade math. *But*, I had stuck my tongue out at the evaluators, shaming the family name in the process.

I'm joking of course. My mother was pretty awesome and really was proud of how I'd done at the evaluation. She had already assumed I was smart. The truth is, every parent thinks his or her child is smart. It's the nature of parenthood. Developmentally I'd done everything early. I'd done everything off kilter though as well. At six months I was uttering my first words. Not "Momma" or "Dadda"... my first word was "dog". At first, it was blown off, even though I was saying it to... *my damn dog*. More words followed soon after. "Dog" was no longer coincidence and finally accepted as my first word. If my being asked to leave Bible Camp was my mother's most embarrassing moment from my childhood, "dog" was her proudest.

I didn't start school that August, but I did start a year early the following fall. School immediately became my favorite place. In school I could ask all the questions I wanted and never be considered "too inquisitive". I could argue my point and never be ridiculed as being a pain or having attitude. I fine-tuned my ability to woo women at every opportunity as well. I easily wrapped each and every teacher I ever had around my finger and put her in my pocket for safekeeping. I don't say this lightly. My ability to get out of a predicament via quick wit and charm has saved my ass on more than one occasion. The sentiment, everything I needed to know, I learned in kindergarten, is true. The only exception being the hair-pulling thing. Girls did *not* like it back then. Now, however, I've never had one complain.

I digress... This chapter may ramble a bit; I'm going to apologize now. The reason being, I hate talking about this. It's difficult to rationalize intellect and not sound like a flaming douchebag. I'm only including this chapter because it'll be relevant later. I need to establish the nature of my thought patterns. I was an intelligent kid. Lots of children are smart. Being intelligent is very different than being smart.

I started school a year early. Two years later, I was recommended for gifted testing by my teacher. She felt I was bored with the current curriculum. She even went as far as to suggest I was making things difficult, simply to entertain myself. My parents agreed, but were reluctant to oblige. My mother had graduated early and felt it had held her back later in life. She did not want to send me down the same path. After the recommended testing, it was discovered that my IQ of 158 and advanced understanding dictated a gifted education program. Starting the following year, one day a week, I attended special classes at our High School. There were six of us from our town of 50,000 who were eligible for the program. I loved it; in fact, it is one of my fondest memories.

When I was in the fourth grade I was retested. The evaluation showed my current comprehension of all academic subjects exceeded high school level. I think this had a lot to do with the set of Encyclopedia Britannica I found myself reading more often than not. The following year, during fifth grade I began taking supplemental high school classes and started working toward early graduation. By this time my mother had resolved to allow it to happen. She apparently resigned that anything else would be holding me back.

Now, looking at the past through more mature eyes, I don't think my parents made the wrong choices. In fact, it should be noted that all of these decisions, regarding my education, were ultimately left up to me. My parents felt that if I was considered intelligent enough to move this fast, I was also intelligent enough to make my own decisions as to how I moved forward. I hate some of those decisions to this day, but I have no one to blame but myself.

I continued down this path until I was able to graduate at fifteen years old. I opted, however, to enter a newly funded advanced education program offered by our school district for a select few students to attend college classes on the state's dime. Each morning I would check into homeroom then leave for college on my own volition. The first year, I hiked through the woods behind our high school to the local community college. This allowed me to walk through the graduation ceremony with my own class, yet gain two years of college credit. At age seventeen, I was a junior at the University of Cincinnati, living on my own and just a few credit hours away from my first degree.

Now that you have the overview of my educational experience, let me explain the significance. I missed out on my childhood. I spent every waking hour reading, studying, going to piano lessons, attending art exhibits, traveling with school programs and watching as all of my friends went through puberty, got their driver's licenses and entered the world of dating. I didn't miss out on the social aspect of my childhood, but being years younger than my peers I was forced to work around my physical drawbacks and talk my way into situations that a child my age should not be accustomed to. I made it out unscathed, but not unaffected. Maturity reached my mind before my body was ready. I was a prepubescent sheep running with wolves. Then I was making the decisions as a teenager that everyone else would put off until they reached well into their twenties. By the time I reached the same age, I was moving forward on life decisions that should have taken place ten years later. Some of which, I regret to this day, but again, I have no one to blame but myself.

The difference between being intelligent and being smart is never more evident than when I play a game of Trivial Pursuit. Intelligence dictates problem solving and aptitude toward recognition of solutions. It is the ability to see patterns and discern thinking outside the normal accepted channels. It is the ability to learn and adapt to new things, techniques and concepts at an advanced rate. Smart is remembering the state capitals and knowing who was the thirtieth President. Smart answers the questions correctly in Trivial Pursuit but much like the game of life, intelligence manipulates the questions so that even the wrong answer gets you a piece of pie. I could survive long enough to find my way out of a woods if my plane ever crashed but I can't tell you where Topeka is or who Carter's Vice President was. Sports? Don't even get me started. I have no idea who plays what, which city has which team or even what sport has any given mascot. It's sad really.

When I was nine years old, my dad bought me a used set of Encyclopedia Britannica. I remember wanting to read them all from cover to cover to absorb the full wealth of knowledge known by man. Instead, I would focus on the things that interested me, most of which, were more about the human brain, physics or what was accepted and known about the universe as a whole. Never once did I sit down and memorize the state capitals.

The older I get, the more unimportant my intelligence becomes. Everyone seems to have stories similar to mine now. The world is not so small anymore. Thirty years ago, my life was confined to the small bubble in Ohio that myself and 50,000 other midwestern conservatives called home. Everything I knew was surrounded on four sides by cornfields. The world wide web was not developed until I was about to graduate college. Nowadays, I can wake up, say hello to my best friend on the west coast, answer a note from another continent and have a meeting with a colleague on the opposite side of the planet... all before my first cup of coffee. The world has become so insignificant and small, intellect is secondary to information. Everything is readily available.

Intelligence is being replaced with Internet savvy.

CHAPTER 7

MATHEMATICS

With a "tsk tsk tsk" and a huff, she giggled to herself and returned to her typewriter. I had at least left an impression. I returned to the task of swinging my legs back and forth below the chair in an attempt to will myself to the playground at school where I should have been at that given moment. I listened closely to the sound of a car speeding up and shifting gears as it attempted to make a yellow light. I looked up and watched the smooth red door across from me open gracefully as the screech of tires outside let me know the light had changed to red sooner rather than later...

Mathematics has always been a comforting concept. Math is near absolute. It rarely changes. 2 + 2 will always equal 4. This is a premise I can get behind. I latch onto things that have resolutions and known borders. Things I cannot explain or resolve with logic frighten me. Mathematics is a means to combat the confusion and frustrations that go with my apeirophobia. When I start to contemplate infinite expansion and the universe in general, I can calm myself with mathematical constants. Prime numbers are a quick and easy fix.

Throughout my life, I've always taken solace in numbers. I've also found serenity through art. Numbers play an important unseen role in what the human eye thinks is beautiful, acceptable and appealing. There is a geometric solution to most visual conundrums. The eye will always travel to a preset focal point. The brain makes these assumptions and the eyes carry them out without us knowing or being conscious of the reason some things just appear to be more attractive than others. People are the same way. No matter what the trend or climate of society in general, certain aspects of human anatomy will always be appealing. There is a perfect facial geometry. These truths are provable and undisputable. Provable and undisputable make me happy.

Not only do I find peace in numbers, I find it in patterns as well. A few years ago I discovered Sudoku. Like everything else I get my hands on, it became an immediate obsession. Finally, I had to force myself to step away. I started seeing patterns where there were none. Spend four to six hours a day solving Sudoku puzzles and your brain will start to see matching numbers in everything from the menu behind the counter at McDonald's to the flashing "No Walk" sign at the corner intersection. This may be a bit of an exaggeration... I hate McDonald's.

In High School we were required to take the Armed Services Vocational Aptitude Battery, or ASVAB. The tests are designed to evaluate newly enlisted service men and women for their abilities and strengths so that the military can better place them in the most effective area of the armed services. Taking the tests in High School, it is presented to the students as a practice test for more important things such as the SAT and ACT. The more tests you take, the easier test taking becomes. Those of us with little or no intention of ever enlisting found the tests pointless and a complete waste of time. We therefore treated them as such.

I cannot take a test and *not* feel as if I'm competing with each and every question for the correct solution. I want to win. I had a hard time blowing off the test. If the armed military flunky had not been standing at the head of the classroom monitoring the students, reminding me how stupid and pointless the tests in fact were, I would have found it impossible to *not* make the most of the test. His smug demeanor and overzealous attitude were just enough to keep my feet firmly planted in the exciting world of making my own decisions.

That is until I reached the mechanical portion of the test where I was given line patterns and asked to complete the code. This timed section designed to test a person's code-breaking ability was relaxing. Because of my nonchalance and obvious lack of respect for both the tests themselves and the armed guard ten feet away, once that portion of the timed test was complete and everyone else moved onto the next section, I did not.

I spent the rest of the allotted time blankly filling in the scan-tron bubbles for the portion that was supposed to be taken then sneaking back to the section with the puzzles I so adored. I've always had a strong urge to push back against authority. Especially when that authority is there for the sole purpose of expressing its perceived legitimacy to the power it feels fit and necessary to portray and not something more productive or positive like actually directing things toward peaceful solutions or protection against harm. That's the nicest way I can say how I really feel. In other words, the prick at the front of the classroom trying his hardest not to pop wood because he has a firearm and camouflage pants was pissing me off by just by being there. I cheated on the test out of pure principle.

It did come back to bite me on the ass. Within a month military recruiters were knocking on my front door, calling the house, even waiting outside my classrooms. At first I thought it was funny. The more persistent they grew, the more annoying it became. I tried everything from a polite brush off to outright rage filled "fuck you's" and spitting. Nothing worked.

One day, leaving my Quantum Mechanics lecture, the professor stopped me. I had argued a principle on overcoming gravity the day before and assumed he was going to try to counter my theory.

The lecture had included a small blurb that no matter how hard you pulled a string, of any length, two bodies under the same duress as the string itself from the gravity of a larger mass could not stretch the string straight without breaking it. Simply put, two people standing on Earth could not, no matter what, pull a string straight between the two of them because the pull of gravity on the center of the string would not allow it. I immediately argued. The obvious solution was to stop attempting to pull the string straight. Taking into consideration the length of the string and the distance between the two people, if you allow the center of the string to meet the pull of gravity then pull until the curve of the string becomes tangent to the curve of the Earth you can pull the string straight. In relation to the curve of the Earth, the string will show slack, but in relation to the endless nothing of space, the string will be... dum dum dum... straight. Math trumping Physics when you look at the larger picture. I win. He did not agree. Although my theory could be shown and demonstrated on paper, the Professor felt my argument only proved that his statement was poorly written. Not incorrect. I agreed, but that didn't change the fact that I was right and he was wrong. I win. Again.

Anyway, I stopped by his desk, the smile already on my face assuming he was going to counter my protest with another pointless argument that I would again be able to quickly shoot down. Instead I was met with, "Travis, there's someone here I'd like you to meet." He turned and I followed him out of the lecture hall into his office where a member of the US Army was waiting. I was immediately pissed.

He introduced himself as Sergeant First Class Willis (it took everything I had to refrain from spouting "whatchatalkinbout?" throughout many parts of the following conversation). He let me know that he was an old friend of my professor. Together they spent the next fifteen minutes attempting to explain the importance of my analytical thinking within certain aspects of the military. I sat in silence. Scratch that, I sat awestruck at the audacity of the ambush. Back and forth they spoke, mentioning things like civil service, civic duty, national security and opportunities beyond my wildest imagination. When they realized that I had completely lost interest, SFC Willis changed tactics.

"What if we allowed you to keep your current hairstyle? If the uniform is a problem, I can have exceptions made there as well."

This snapped me back to the conversation. I'd never even known it was possible to get away with such nonsense within our military. "What? Why would the Army let me do that?" I asked.

"That's what we're trying to explain to you," my professor interrupted, "your uncanny ability to see patterns and break codes is *that* important."

I was thoroughly confused and my face must have shown it.

"Your test results on the Armed Services Vocational Aptitude Battery were among the highest we've ever received under the Numerical Operations portion of testing. You're a natural code-breaker. No one, NO ONE gets as many completed as you had. And correct. After looking into your academic history, we feel this is a perfect fit for you." SFC Willis was on the edge of his seat by then, thinking he was breaking ground with me.

I started to explain that I'd cheated but thought better of it. I had no idea what would happen if I were actually caught doing what I'd done. I started to regret my spiteful actions and just wanted out of the office. "I have class. Thank you but no thank you." I got up, gathered my stuff and started for the door.

A shiny, perfectly laced, black boot blocked my path. THIS really pissed me off. I stared at it for a moment, deciding how to proceed. "One minute more, son. How can we convince you the importance of getting you on board?"

I looked up at the pawn and offered the following, "If you were intelligent enough to look into my academic history,

I'd have hoped you were intelligent enough to realize that I'd never allow myself to become part of an organization that prides itself on imposing its importance over the free will of others. Hence, move your fucking foot." He did.

The following day, when I arrived home from school, there were two black Chevrolet Blazers parked out front, both donning government plates. I walked around the side of the house and up the back steps, hoping to avoid another incident like yesterday. As I opened the back door, my mother was closing the front.

"I heard what you told that recruiter yesterday," my father said over his shoulder as he continued to stare out the peephole of our front door. "I'm proud of you."

I stopped and dropped my bag in the chair. "He wasn't a recruiter, he was *Sergeant First Class Willis of the United States Army*, here to offer me the world." I mocked a salute.

"Your father told them you were a bed wetter." My mother crossed her arms and sneered at my dad.

"What?" I laughed.

"Your uncle told me that it was a surefire way to get them to leave you alone. I figured I'd give it a shot. They didn't believe me at first." Dad chuckled.

"Oh, he made sure to make the story VERY convincing," my mother added, "even talking about how it's held you back since you were a child."

Just for the record, I am not a bed wetter...

Just for the record, they never came around or called again.

CHAPTER 8

INNER VOICE

"Travis, she's ready for you now." I took a deep breath and hopped down off of the chair. I grabbed my coat and walked toward the open door. The woman I approached was new so I took a moment to take her all in. I walked a little slower and noticed I could see the top edge of her stocking peeking out from under the hem of her skirt. I sped up, realizing that I was staring. As I grew nearer, I looked up and saw the expression on her face. No smile, she'd caught me looking. I offered a simple yet innocent, "Hi." That must have done it. "Hi. I'm sure you know where you're going by now, huh?"

She smiled. "Yep," I answered with delight as I turned on my heel and walked backwards down the hall, making sure she saw the smile on my face before she entered her own office...

If you're still reading, you've figured out by now that there are a lot of strange things rattling around up in my head. I have a plethora of issues. Scratch that. I have a plethora of problems. The truth is, I'm not the only one in my family like this. When I was nine a close relative succumbed to her own fears and was diagnosed schizophrenic. Institutionalized at age 35 of her own accord, she would eventually be considered stable, put on a cocktail of meds and shipped out to live on her own among the normal folks making up the rest of society.

I need to make it very clear, she has always been one of the most important people in my life. As far back as I can remember, she is in almost every one of my most vivid memories. Most people have that one influential grownup from their childhood who treated them like the adult they were going to become instead of the kid they were. For some it was an older brother or sister, for others it was a young aunt or uncle. Sometimes it was a neighbor or a stepparent. She has always been there for me and I hope that one day, if needed, I can be there for her.

A few years later, while living on her own, she was traumatized outside her apartment. The incident sent her spiraling back into the confines of her head. A few weeks later she was in the middle of her shift at work, turned to her boss and asked for someone to replace her. She admitted not feeling good, went to her locker, grabbed her purse and drove straight to the hospital. I remember my parents coming into my bedroom that night and telling me that she had checked herself back into the hospital. "It was a good thing though," they'd told me, "because it meant that she was well enough to recognize the problem."

I was allowed to visit her just once while she was in residence at the clinic. We walked through the front doors and were met by an invisible wall of antiseptic cleaner and bleach, the quintessential smell of hospital. My dad escorted me to the visitor's area where she would be waiting for us. The smell is what I remember most. It wasn't that it was "dirty" as much as it was "too clean". The kind of clean that smells like its purpose is to hide something much more offensive. All around were other patients, shuffling to and fro harmlessly, in a narcotic haze. We've all seen psych wards in films and on television. I'm here to report that in my hometown, the psych ward did not disappoint. Instead it was as if it was designed specifically to keep up the accepted appearances set forth by "One

Flew Over the Cuckoo's Nest".

We were directed to a table in the middle of a sunlit room. The tables were filled with loved ones there to see drooling family members, wish them well and then get up and get the fuck out. It was a roomful of necessary obligations. I had a hard time focusing on the visit with the drama commencing all around me.

"Hi little man," she greeted me as she stood up and accepted a hug from my dad.

"Hi," I answered shyly.

"How are you doing?" my Dad asked.

She pulled my chair around the table nearest hers. "I'm glad you came to see me. I wanted to explain some things to you." My father seemed very nervous. He gave her a look that reminded her that she was talking to an eleven year old. She considered for a moment, and then continued. "Do you know why I'm in here?"

I looked at my dad, not wanting to upset her with an incorrect answer. "Go ahead, Travis." He encouraged my response having discussed the situation with me on the way to the hospital.

I answered tentatively, "You're in here because you're hearing voices again?"

"That's right. You're so smart." She spoke slow and deliberate. Thinking back on it now, it was more likely whatever medication they had her on more so than her condescension toward my adolescent age. "The voices in my head are not my own. Sometimes they are nice and don't bother me. Sometimes they help me. Sometimes they tell me to do bad things. That's how I knew it was time to get some help."

"Are they helping you?" My dad asked.

"Yes," she answered. "I think I'm doing much better already."

"What kind of bad things do the voices tell you to do?" I asked before I was able to stop myself.

She never answered the question, instead she showed me the ashtray she'd made earlier that day and showed us the bedroom she was in. Because she was a voluntary resident, her accommodations were pretty nice. Shortly after, my Dad and I left. The ride home was silent until we reached our driveway.

"She's going to be fine ya know." He stared out the windshield at the garage door in front of us. "They're taking good care of her." He was talking to me, but the words were meant for his own benefit.

It didn't take long for her to come home from the hospital. She's been living with relatives ever since. I assume she continues to have bouts with her issues, but to look into her eyes and see her smile, you'd never know. She is, and always has been, one of my heroes. I still remember that day, visiting her in the hospital as a kid. The courage that she had to have to first admit there was a problem and second, to seek the necessary help to deal with it has always inspired me. She's an amazing woman both despite her issues and because of them.

I fear that as I get older, I'll start to follow in her footsteps. I am now 35, the age she was when she was first hospitalized. It's a heavy weight to bear. Then, I look at my boys, both of whom are testing in the 150+ IQ range, and I wonder if I make it through this life unscathed, will they?

Whenever I'm seen for my issues or we're filling out paperwork for my kids there is a question about family history, mental illness and hereditary disorders. I hate that box. I don't hear voices. Yet. I hear one. My own. I think. He's my companion; my co-pilot; my conscious.

It's not so much that I talk to him, as it is that he talks to me. He is me... or so I think. I'm not sure if what I experience is out of the ordinary or if it's completely normal and I'm just looking into something too deep. How do you ask someone to explain how he or she thinks and what their inner dialogue is like without coming across as totally nuts?

During the summer of my tenth birthday, I became self aware of the conversations that went on within my own head. I don't know any other way to describe it. One day, I was a normal kid (normal with insomnia, apeirophobia and an antagonistic imaginary accomplice known as The Shadow Man... ok, not so normal). The next day, I had an inner monologue. I think it had always been there but I was too hyper or too preoccupied to recognize it for what it was. It wasn't until I sat across the table in that sterile hospital and heard the words, "the voices in my head are not my own," that I started to worry that there may be more going on than I was able to comprehend.

Sigmund Freud's structural model of the psyche says there are three parts of the psychic apparatus: the Id, ego and super-ego. The Id is the dark, inaccessible part of our personality that drives us toward our instinctual desires. The ego is the mediator between Id and reality. It drives our life through common sense and reason. The super-ego aims for perfection through morality and the influence of the world around it. The super-ego is the portion of the psyche that acts as the father, the patriarch and the decision maker.

After discovering my co-pilot, I began to rethink Freud's concept of the psyche as it had been previously explained to me by my set of Encyclopedia Britannica. Freud did address the aspects of the psyche in terms of a power struggle between pleasure, morality and order. How do other people wage this war within their own life? Maybe I'm not different than the next guy, only more aware.

I have Rene Descartes' "I Think Therefore I Am" tattooed down my left arm. The meaning of this quote is very important to me. It keeps me sane. It reminds me that no matter what, my co-pilot is with me. He is me. I am me. Whether or not you all exist is irrelevant to the world I have in my head.

And believe me, the world in my head is a fantastic place.

CHAPTER 9

SUICIDE

I turned around just as I reached the end of the hall. Face to face with the door that led me to salvation, I brushed my hair with my hands and adjusted my shirt. I wasn't trying to impress; it was nervous behavior. I hated going into this office. The questions always seemed to point the finger back at me. I felt as if I had to defend myself the entire time I was on the couch. I did not like being the object of attention either. Once I went through those doors, I became a guinea pig. I reached for the handle and hesitated. I checked my hair once more and pulled my shirt out only to tuck it back in.

Before I could finish, the door opened in front of me. There she stood, waiting. "I was beginning to get worried that you weren't going to come have lunch with me," she said as she looked down on me from atop her menacing height. Her voice whispered the words with annoyance shrouded by the caress of compassion. I was convinced. She wanted me to break...

Eventually everyone contemplates suicide at some point in his or her life.

Ok, I don't really know this for a fact, but I can make an educated guess all the same and still feel pretty fucking confident that the results will be correct. It may have been a simple fleeting thought. Even a glimpse at a future without you in it should qualify. What about toying with the notion of "if I were to die, would anyone miss me?" or "I'd rather be dead than face this problem"?

Eventually everyone contemplates suicide at some point in his or her life.

I am no exception. There were many nights when the thought of ending it all seemed so much easier than facing another day. At times, my inherent inability to accept failure or defeat may have been the only thing that kept the thoughts from becoming reality. Sometimes, when the apeirophobia and insomnia pushed me to the edge of rational behavior, I would play out full scenarios in my mind and decide how suicide would best be undertaken. When I was young, I would take into consideration what it would do to my parents. Would they blame themselves? Would my sister be able to move on without a stigma of being the girl with the brother who killed himself? Would my death make things difficult for them?

After I had my own children, the thoughts changed course completely. No longer would I consider the effects of the suicide on my loved ones. The scenarios became about making my suicide look like an accident. A murder? After all, I've got life insurance for a reason right? If I'm not around, my family should at least get a big check to help them forget about how much of a burden I was. Could I put it in my will that the life insurance payout be made into one of those giant cardboard checks you see on television? That would make the whole event festive. Who doesn't want a giant cardboard check?

The planning and meticulous skill that would be required to pull off a suicide that is ruled as an accident or murder seemed more like a game than a way out. The time that would be involved in order to make it realistic would probably be a good thing. Most of the plots I developed over the years would last upward of six months. By the time the suicide was actually at hand, I would have either snapped out of the funk, slept or discovered multiple holes through which the plan would inevitably give the ruse away.

The most effective way to kill yourself and get away with it would seem to be a car accident; slammed brakes, a swerve to avoid an imaginary animal that frolics off after the car careens through the guardrail and off the bridge to the icy cold river below where you drown from panic and shock. The bridge would have to be high enough to ensure the crash. The water would have to be deep enough to ensure drowning. The guardrail would need to be weak enough to give way when smashed into. The car would need to be large enough to not fold under pressure. The worst possible outcome would be surviving with serious unrecoverable injuries. The risk would likely not be worth the reward.

The most extravagant way to kill yourself and get away with it would have to be a failed kidnapping resulting in death by exposure. This one would require an extremely long time to plan. First you'd have to purchase all necessary materials with cash at various times in various places, along with other inconspicuous items. Buying 24" zip ties two days before you go missing would be a huge red flag. You would have to scout out a large enough wooded area to make getting lost within it plausible. The best time of year to make this solution work would be deep in the icy cold heart of winter. Snow and ice on the ground would make things go quicker as well. On the day of the deed, you'd need to be about twenty miles from home. Just far enough to give you the time allotted for your escape yet close enough to make the escape seem irrational. Make a phone call to loved ones letting them know that you have a slow leak in your tire. You are going to swap it for the spare and then head home soon after. No need to send help, it won't take long and you already have it underway. Then, pull over and make like you're changing a tire. If anyone stops, stand up and brush your hands off, look up and offer a, "thank you, but I just finished." Next toss your phone on the side of the interstate, jump back in the car and turn around. Drive responsible. You don't want to get pulled over for something silly. Last, make sure you put on sunglasses and a large hat, just in case you are picked up by any cameras.

Drive directly to a secluded access road connected to the

previously scouted wooded area. Leave the car parked with a door open or ajar. Make sure the car is out of sight enough not to look conspicuous but not so well hidden as it's never found. Grab your tools and leave everything else in the car. Leave your wallet (remove a family photo first), leave your keys and leave your coat, even your shoes. Remember, you are about to kill yourself; comfort is secondary. Slip on the shoes you purchased months before with cash that are three sizes too large and make your way around the car several times, then tread off into the woods.

Once inside, far enough from your car to cover your own tracks, it's time to make the hard decisions. First, take off as many clothes as you can to ensure your eventual demise. Burn the clothes in a small clearing, leaving your lighter in the center of the fire. Fold up the picture of your family that you pulled out of your wallet back at the car. Grasp it in your hand and do not let go. Use the 24" zip ties, also purchased months before, to bind your wrists. You don't have to wrap them together necessarily, but the more uncomfortable the better. Believability is the key here. Actually making the final scene seem as improbable as possible for you to have done this to yourself is going to be required.

Run, run, run.

Run until you can't breathe anymore, then run some more. Trip, fall, hit your head on a rock... then run some more. Finally, you'll find yourself out of breath and longing for the relief death will bring. Sit down in the snow. Curl up. Give up.

Ta-da. Suicide accomplished. Life insurance remains intact. You will undoubtedly be remembered as the guy who, even at death's door, tried desperately to make his way to safety with only a crumpled picture of his family offering support.

These are the types of things I contemplate and argue over in my head when I should be sleeping.

CHAPTER 10

A HELPING HAND

She moved aside and allowed me entrance to her inner sanctum. I stepped lively and took my place on the couch per my weekly routine. She shut the door and strode around her desk, picking up a brown paper sack on her way to sit beside me on the couch. I watched as she opened the bag and placed its contents on two paper plates, evenly distributed despite our obvious difference in mass and apparent hunger. "Have you forgotten my rules so soon?" she asked. Without a word of protest, I jumped up off of the couch and ran to the sink in her private bathroom. Stretching on extended toes, I let loose the hot water and proceeded to wash my hands thoroughly. Turning on the faucet was much easier than turning it off so I resorted to teetering on the edge of the sink abreast the fulcrum of my favorite nylon Star Wars belt...

My parents were independent in their childrearing. They liked to think. Looking back, however, I could paint a much different picture. My parents sought regular council at every turn: from my mother's pastor, to my pediatrician, to God, to family and finally ending with my very first therapist. The problem was always trying to explain something that I'm only now starting to fully understand. My issues all come back to one thing. When what troubles you is not being able to explain something, explaining *that* becomes ridiculously pointless and frustrating.

Every attempt for resolution was met with more questions rather than answers. My fears and anxiety were skirted, ignored or rationalized as something I'd eventually outgrow. The most commonly presented solution was faith in God. The problem with apeirophobia and the solution of finding faith is that if you're truly apeirophobic, the concept of a higher power simply contradicts the fear itself. If I believed in God, that would be the answer to all of the questions my brain refuses to forget. God is not an answer, it's an excuse. For anyone to tell someone with a fear of reality without boundaries that there is a magical answer that only accepting an all knowing, all seeing, all powerful deity that you cannot prove exists, does by way of fault, exist, makes it painfully obvious that they DID NOT FUCKING UNDERSTAND THE PROBLEM IN THE FIRST PLACE.

Therapy, on the other hand, was more of a controlled question and answer session geared toward making me find the solution myself through a deep seeded search of my thought process. It quickly became more a game than anything to my adolescent sense of anarchy and mischief. I found it very entertaining to lie to my therapists to see how they reacted. They'd ask a question, I'd give a bullshit answer, then see what kind of a question it volleyed. I would lay awake at night thinking of possible scenarios specifically created to fuck with their delicate concept of what was going on in my head.

I'm not saying therapy didn't help. It did. I'm just saying that the only thing that has ever really done anything positive for me has been self-expression. Recently I've made strides toward personal harmony by taking a leap into the world of microblogging. Putting my feelings into words is something I've done for decades, but allowing others to read my personal confessions has produced results I wasn't expecting. The more I divulged, the more memories I unlocked, filling in mental holes I've kept locked away since I was a child. Completion of the novel you're still reading (you are still reading right?) will be my ultimate confession.

Now that I've thoroughly explained the truths behind my life and the way I think, it's time to paint the story, from the beginning, as I remembered it. There will be holes. There will be confusion. There will be enlightened wisdom and revelations.

Forget what you know and enjoy the show.

PART II

RIDDLED WITH HOLES

CHAPTER 11

BY THE GRACE OF GOD

Upon reentering her office, I noticed her watching me. She always watched me with evaluating eyes. I could feel her comparing my every movement and response, looking for a meaning that may or may not even be there. I could feel her plotting. "You look as if you're deep in something cerebral. A penny for your thoughts?" she asked. I slowed my walk, purposely modifying my pace just to see her reaction. What would it mean if I walked bow legged? How about backwards? What if I skipped across the room and took a shit on the carpet? How would her textbooks define that? "A penny huh? With what my mom is paying you, that's all you can afford to spare?" Damn, I was clever. She huffed and handed me my plate. "Thank you," I continued politely. She smiled, pleased with my manners. The first fifteen minutes were always spent over a plate of kettle-cooked potato chips, peanut butter sandwiches, an apple and a carton of chocolate milk...

"Hurry up and finish your Cheerios, Mr. Wick is going to be ready soon." My mother flitted about the kitchen like a moth fighting for purchase on a porch light. "You still need to brush your teeth!"

Today was my first day of Bible Camp. My mother's church was offering the service for two weeks, in the heat of July, without air conditioning. Most governments would have considered this cruel and unusual punishment. I hopped down from the table and proceeded to get ready. My mother had laid out my clothes last night flat on my bedroom floor. She apparently wanted me to appear as though someone responsible had dressed me. Button up shirt and khaki pants. Did she not realize that I'd be melting by mid morning? I looked at the silk-screened Yoda t-shirt and striped shorts sitting on my chair with longing and dismay. Reluctantly, I chose my battle wisely and buttoned up the plaid dress shirt with a sigh.

I'd never attended church before that day. My mother went regularly, but I had always been permitted to stay home with my father instead. The last few weeks I'd been asking questions that my mother could not answer. Questions like, "How can there be a God and your religion be right if there are lots of religions? Is everyone else wrong?" and "How do you know there is a heaven? Just because someone tells you to jump off of a bridge, you don't have to do it." She wasn't very happy with me. My father had found it funny. She did not. After a few weeks of badgering her without remorse, she took up the quandary with her pastor. He was the one who had suggested she spring for enrollment in the Bible Camp. He assured her that all of my questions could be answered by studying the good word of the Holy Bible.

Before this day I had been fascinated with Chaos Theory. I was convinced that each and every action undertaken by each and every person had repercussions felt across the span of human kind. A boy in Guatemala eats a corn taco and a bird in Phoenix flies directly into a window. There must be a greater connection between all living things than just the random collision of molecules resulting in an acceptable collage of life. Like ripples in a lake, each initial change in condition affects every wave that the initial wave touches, changing each wave each changed wave touches, and so on and so on. Chaotic systems cannot be determined or predicted but they can be manipulated. Making changes in your life that you would normally not make can change everything for everyone.

I began to make changes to my behavior on purpose just to change the course of human kind. I began second guessing every action for fear of how it would affect the rest of the world. From this obsession I began to concern myself with faith and religion. My mother's beliefs contradicted the mathematical validity of quantum chaos. Faith in a greater good allowed her to believe that everything happened for a reason. By this measure, when I decided to throw away my peanut butter sandwich, even though I was still hungry, the decision was not my own. That decision was either already made as a part of my destiny or the outcome of such decision did not affect the greater good so it was rendered moot. My decision did not affect the rest of mankind, only my own hunger two hours later.

There were too many factors in life. Too many beliefs and structures of thought for any one person to be more correct than the next. More and more I realized that all religious beliefs were nothing more than an answer to whatever question plagued people. They became for most a crutch. I was expected to accept one and move on. The questions I had been asking would all be answered as soon as I accepted a larger notion and allowed it to trickle down as truth. I ask a lot of questions. It's in my nature. Accepting something without proof is not.

A few hours later, I found myself in the basement of the church, huddled around a long table with a dozen other five to eight year olds. The ceiling was incredibly low in the basement room. I noticed that the teacher's hair was charged with static and magnetically clinging to the low tiles as she walked up and down the length of our table, passing out stickers as we colored our pages with pictures of our family and the church.

"And who is in that picture with you?" she asked as she passed behind me. She was already moving on to the next student when I answered.

"That's me with Jesus and Buddha." She paused, hearing what I said, but *not hearing* at the same time. The day came to an end and I headed through the parking lot toward my mother's LTD Station Wagon with a piece of paper clutched in my hand.

"What is that? Did you have fun?" my mother asked as I approached the car with my six-year-old neighbor in tow.

"This is my homework. I need help looking up all of these passages in the Bible when we get home." I wasn't happy about the homework.

"Did you get lots of homework too, Joshua?" my mother asked my neighbor as we got into the car.

"Nope, just Travis. He made Miss Embry mad. She said he asks too many questions." Joshua was a little tattle telling pain in my ass.

"I *did not*. She just wasn't smart enough to answer the few questions I *did* ask."

"What kinds of questions did you ask?" My mother already sounded defensive.

"Normal stuff, like why are Christian's right and Muslim's wrong? Why do Adam and Eve have belly buttons in our coloring book if God created them? *THEN*, she was very upset that I colored Jesus brown. I don't even want to talk about that." My mother just looked at me in the rear view mirror, visibly distraught at my first day experience.

That night we spent what felt like a lifetime looking up each verse in the Bible suggested by Miss Embry. My mother attempted to explain what each one meant to me but it was painfully obvious that she was half confused herself. Eventually we both opted for a break and a "do you understand?" followed by, "Sure" and a sigh. Homework complete.

The next day, I presented my paper, signed by my mother, to Miss Embry. "Were you and your mom able to shed some light on those blasphemous questions?" she asked.

"Nope. There are no answers in this book." I took my seat after I handed her the paper I'd filled out explaining what I'd read in each suggested verse.

She took the paper, looked it over briefly and chose to carry on class rather than address my continued quizzical comments. Instead of engaging me in a heated debate over every question I brought to the table, Miss Embry chose to ignore my raised hand. I held it higher. She continued to ignore. I added "Miss Embry! Miss Embry! Miss Embry!" to each raised hand. She continued to ignore.

The day concluded so far out of her control that she left twenty minutes before the end of class. The study was resumed by my mother's pastor, who spent the final moments discussing with us the importance of good manners and knowing our place with Miss Embry. As parents arrived to pick up their little ones, I was held back. "I need to speak with your mother." I was then sent out to the car to retrieve my mom. This couldn't be good. Joshua and I, as per yesterday, jumped into the back of the car, except this time, to wait for my mother's return.

Twenty minutes passed before my mom silently slid back into the front seat. We drove straight home, bypassing the Dairy Barn where lunch had been promised. Joshua and I protested, but my mother continued her homeward course unabashed by our whining.

When my mother and I walked into the house, I was asked to take a seat at the kitchen table. After a few minutes, my mother came in and the interrogation began.

"Are you *trying* to embarrass me?" she asked in a voice laden with accusation.

"No. What did I do?" I was dumbfounded.

"I was asked not to bring you back tomorrow." She sat down across from me at the booth my family used as a kitchen table. I must have smiled because her voice climbed an octave in disgust, "That's exactly what you wanted, isn't it?"

I stopped. I knew when it was best to just keep my mouth shut. No matter how I answered at this point, my mother was determined to make this my fault. There was no point in arguing. I may as well let her punch herself out.

"Answer me," she continued. "No, don't answer that. I don't want to know. I just hope you realize how this makes me look. I went to the pastor seeking help and you made me out to be the fool."

Still I sat silent. "Just look innocent," I thought to myself.

"Nothing? You have nothing to say?" She tapped her foot for a heartbeat. "No, I don't want to hear it. Do you know what the pastor told me? He said that you were going out of your way to upset Miss Embry by asking her blasphemous questions and ridiculing her as being naïve and unintelligent because she was unable... nay, *UNWILLING* to give you an answer that you couldn't argue about. I know you're skeptical, Travis, and smart... but this was about good manners and being polite. One day you'll learn when being right is not as important as being kind." She huffed and walked out of the kitchen leaving me sitting alone at the tiny laminated table contemplating what I'd done.

I never returned to Bible Camp. I never returned to the church in any capacity in fact. Not until my uncle was married years later, did I even break the threshold of a building of worship. My mother has always blamed it on my need to ask questions rather than have faith. I'd like to blame it on Miss Embry for being a self-righteous jackass unwilling to mix it up with a kindergartener.

CHAPTER 12

THE TRIGGER

We ate in silence. I'd make sure to check her progress out of my peripheral after every bite. I didn't want her to think I was beginning to like her or that I was letting my guard down just because she was playing on my desire for food. "Is it good?" she asked. I nodded and mumbled an agreement through a mouthful of bread and sticky peanut butter. At first I would eat the sandwich, then the apple and finish with the chips. After a while, I thought it would be interesting to mix things up a bit. I'd eat everything backwards for a few weeks. Then sometimes I'd eat a little of each or in no particular order whatsoever, sporadic and without pattern. Anything I could do to deliberately throw off her evaluation of my current mental state, I found devilishly fun. "Would you like something different for a change?" she asked as I popped the last kettle chip into my mouth. "...for next week I mean." I crunched the chip slowly, and then turned to face her, "How about steak?" She laughed then retorted, "Peanut butter it is." Ok, maybe I did like her a little bit. "Did you bring your sleep journal?" she asked as she gathered our discarded plates and napkins. I reached into my bag and pulled out the ragged red notebook I'd been writing in every morning for the last few months...

I always found myself conflicted when a friend spent the night. Part of me wanted to stay in my room and do stupid childhood things like tell ghost stories and talk about which girls at school we wanted to kiss behind the pine trees at the edge of the playground. Another part of me hated pretending to be interested in playing with action figures and the Chicago Bulls or Bears or whatever sports franchise was popular at the time. It usually seemed easier to spend the night in my room alone, reading, than going through the motions of childhood. I did have friends and truly did enjoy hanging out and doing kid type things, but often, it was just too much. I needed my space to brood. Tonight was one of those nights.

Bored with the thousandth game of Pac-Man on my new Atari 2600 (bought and paid for with blood, sweat and tears... and allowance... and report card money) I talked my best friend, Nate, into heading downstairs to see what movie my parents were watching. I mystified him with tales of horror films and comedies ripe with nudity and foul language so he was nothing less than excited. We snuck down the stairs and spied the television through dimly lit banister rails. It appeared to be an international tale of intrigue staring the always debonair, James Bond.

"They'll let us watch if we want," I said in a whispered hush. Nate nodded approval so we stood and snuck into the living room. Tip toes and exaggerated steps brought us up to the neck of my mother in ninja-like silence.

"RAAAWWWRRR!" we yelled in unison, scaring my mother into throwing her bowl of jiffy pop onto the shag carpet. My mother was, and still is, the easiest and most rewarding victim of an impromptu "Boo!" Dad complained, she laughed and we helped pick up the strewn kernels before taking a seat in front of the coffee table to watch the movie.

"It just started boys. You haven't missed anything yet." My dad never budged from his chair as mom jumped up to make another batch of popcorn for herself and the newly added second graders sitting a few feet from the 25" floor model Zenith.

I watched the screen as an American capsule hung innocently in the vacuum of outer space while an astronaut floated nearby tethered by an umbilical cord attached to the hull. "Hawaii to Jupiter 16. Repeat, Hawaii to Jupiter 16. There is an unidentified object on our scope closing fast."

"We see nothing. Can you give me a bearing?" the astronaut said over a static filled communications channel.

"Appears to be coming up fast from astern," came flight control's reply.

"Hey, now I see it. It's another spacecraft! Repeat! It's another spacecraft!" A new silver ship approached from the left…

"Flight Control, it's coming right at us. The front is opening up! I repeat! The front is opening up! It's coming right at us!"

The silver ship spread its jaws and slowly swallowed the American capsule. In the background flight control squawked warnings and spewed pointless requests for updates on what was happening. "Are you receiving? You're breaking up. Come in please, over. Jupiter 16… you're breaking up. Over… Hawaii… are you receiving?..."

"My lead line! It's cut –" The silver ship closed around the capsule, clipping the astronaut's lifeline in its giant metal beak. The astronaut's plea for help was cut short the moment his tether was snipped. His lifeless body floated off into the cold depths of outer space.

Where would he stop if he floated off into the abyss of nothingness? Would he just float forever? Is there an end to space? Where are we and what is all of this? How can there be no end to the universe? I began to have trouble breathing. My chest felt tight. The sound of my surging blood filled my ears like the house was suddenly under high tide.

"Jack, he's choking!" my mother yelled at my father as she

dumped her popcorn for a second time trying to snatch me up across the top of the coffee table. My vision blurred and black started to fill in behind the unfocussed haze that used to be my living room.

Soon there was nothing but the cold black of outer space. My body floated into the abyss.

I've never returned.

CHAPTER 14

THE AFTERMATH

"How have you been sleeping?" she asked. She always asked. I had finally resorted to a simple look that answered the question for me. "I'll take that as no changes." She picked up the red notebook lying beside me on the couch and began to flip through to the last entry. "I fell asleep while I was getting my hair cut. He slipped and nicked my scalp when my head nodded forward. Wanna see?" I bent over and started to inspect my scalp with my fingers, looking for the tender scab that a pair of razor sharp scissors had created. "Did you have to have stitches?" she seemed mildly

concerned, more skeptical than sympathetic. I was silent for a few moments more before I located the rough edge of the wound with my fingertip. I winced as I scratched the cut accidentally. She leaned over, observed the scab and sat back with a low whistle. "What day was that?" I smoothed my hair back to a presentable part and answered, "Tuesday I think. No, Monday." She laughed again. "This is what I want you to write in your journal." She said it with a smile, but emphasized her every word with a finger tap to the beaten red cover...

The next few weeks, I found myself lost in thought throughout the day. I also suffered more frequent panic attacks. They were never quite as severe as the first but were intense each on their own. My parents were concerned with my wellbeing, don't get me wrong, but the moment it was explained to them that what had happened was a panic attack, the seed of doubt was planted. No matter what, in the back of their mind it could all be summed up to behavioral issues. The hardest part was trying to convince them that the fear was real and not a cry for help. At times I tried to will it to be so, anything, just to find peace in my head.

When I was young, it was more difficult to understand how anyone could get through their day without stopping to worry about the same things that plagued me. As I grew older, my disbelief turned to jealousy. I wanted more than anything to lie down at night, close my eyes, and peacefully drift off to sleep like everyone else seemed to do. The ignorant bliss that radiated from those around me was like a metaphorical fuck you. When my mother asked if I had slept the night before, I was honest. She would frown, voice her concern and send me on my way. Playing into my fear would only make it worse. Their initial strategy to correct the issue was an obvious choice to downplay and ignore. To their credit, they made a valiant effort.

The honesty ultimately became pointless. I started to lie about the sleep. "Oh, yeah! I slept just fine! I even dreamt about the ice cream truck coming, but the driver was Mr. Wilson from school. He asked me if I wanted to ride the roller coaster, except it was full of teddy bears. All the teddy bears wanted me to take them on an adventure so we sailed out to an island to look for buried treasure. It was a weird dream by golly." That seemed more normal than what had actually happened the night before.

Even though I was attempting to convince everyone through my words that I was sleeping and doing just fine, as soon as I started to have a panic attack at the grocery store or I passed out in the backseat of the car on the way to Cub Scouts, my aim at normalcy was deemed a failure. The sleep deprivation and panic attacks started to take their toll quickly. I was only able to catnap two to three hours each day. I found myself sneaking sleep when I needed it most. If I attempted to sleep in my bed at night, my brain was met by a collision of questions and worry. However, I *could* fall fast asleep if I felt my eyes getting heavy throughout the day. I stopped fighting and just succumbed to the sensation. They were never effective or long naps, but they were enough to take the edge off. I began a new routine of getting out of bed at 6:29am, before my alarm was scheduled to go off, and sneaking into the bathroom past my parent's room. I'd lock the door and turn on the shower, hot water and steam helped. I'd grab a large bath towel and curl up on the floor over the heater vent. The warm air would collect under the towel and wrap around me like an insulated hug. Focusing on the shower, the heat and the need for sleep allowed me to slip away for a while. As soon as my dad would knock on the door, I'd jump up, wet my hair, shut off the shower and rush to unlock the door. Looking back now, I wonder what he assumed I was doing in there. Surely not napping.

I started to abandon all efforts to sleep at night in lieu of naps throughout the day. They never lasted longer than twenty minutes so I didn't feel the need to set an alarm or take any grand precautions. When I felt the ability to nod off coming on, I took the appropriate steps to make it so. Frequent bathroom runs under the guise of a dramatic fit of stomach cramps worked quite well.

For a while…

I remember feeling as if I was back in control. I could handle this. Everything was going to be ok. Then my Mom called me down to the kitchen from my bedroom. The note I'd brought home from my second grade teacher was *not* a request for help at the Thanksgiving Party like I had assumed. My teacher was requesting a conference to discuss my "strange behavior."

"What strange behavior is Mrs. Defoe referring to?" My mother stood in the doorway, flipping the note with her fingernail. "What should I be aware of before I go in there? I do *not* like surprises?"

"I have no idea what you're talking about," I said. It was the truth. In my mind, everything was going according to plan. I had no "strange behavior" to be concerned about.

"Obviously something is going on or she wouldn't have requested I call her to set something up. Go back to your room and before supper tonight I want you to come down here, on your own, and explain to me why you think I may be heading into your school tomorrow evening." She turned and went back to the chicken and dumplings she was preparing for dinner. I hated dumplings.

"Maybe if I just went to my room and hid I could at least get out of the dumplings," I'd thought to myself. Out loud, I said, "I really don't know, but I'll think about it, mom." I turned and ran back upstairs. I knew what she was talking about. How many times had I been going to the bathroom each day? It didn't seem like much, but maybe it was.

The next night, my mother went to meet Mrs. Defoe despite my continued plea of ignorance about the point of the meeting. I sat at home, with my father acting as my babysitter, stewing over the discussion taking place on the other side of town. When mom returned home, she immediately took my sister and laid her down for the night. Then she called another family meeting. Mrs. Defoe had voiced concern over my bathroom breaks, no big shocker there. Apparently, the frequency of trips was greater than I'd thought.

"Your son is taking ten to fifteen bathroom breaks everyday." My mother directed the statement to my father without taking her eyes off of me. "She seemed to think that we may be dealing with... an issue of..." she broke off.

"What?" my dad asked.

My mother leaned over and whispered into my father's ear behind a cupped hand. I watched as his eyes grew twice their norm before narrowing at the temple into a stifled laugh. "Fifteen times a day?!" He shouted through a giggle. "There's no way. He'd have arthritis by now."

My mom turned back to me, the look in her eyes all but swallowed my father's laughter and replaced it with fire. "I hardly think we're ready for that discussion. I think we're dealing with something else all together." She turned back to my father now, "I wish you'd shut up. I had to sit there and hear that from HIS TEACHER for God's sake. How do you answer an accusation like that?"

"Better you than me," my dad continued, "I'd have never been able to do it with a straight face." He must have seen the anger in her eyes or felt the mood in the room darken because he followed with an apology and sat quietly for the remainder of the conversation.

"Why are you going to the bathroom fifteen times a day?" my mother asked the question as if it were the opening line in a murder interrogation. In my mind I heard, "where were you the night the butler was murdered?" I needed an alibi.

"I feel like I have to go to the bathroom a lot. I guess." I answered before thinking it through. The following day I was in the waiting room of our pediatrician being seen for a bladder infection. It was at this office visit that my carefully created persona and skillfully crafted sleep detours started to unravel.

CHAPTER 15

BAIT AND SWITCH

I sat silently, pondering the creases in the back of my thumb, pretending to ignore her as she flipped through my journal. Some weeks I wrote more, some less. A couple months back I'd written nonsense just to see if she was reading it or not. I first added a sentence in the middle of a dream recollection to see if she'd say anything or give away whether or not she saw it. "I hope she isn't reading this because if she is she'll know that I dream about her without clothes on and I made this all up just to have an excuse to come see her." She'd never acknowledged the sentence so the next week I tried it again, this time more risqué. Week after week, I'd ramped up the intensity and severity of my asides until she'd finally put the spiral notebook down and sighed. She had rubbed her forehead with her left hand, kneading her temples between her thumb and middle finger. "Yes, I do read it all, my dear. Each week I read every word. You can stop with the vulgarity now. Please. At first it was cute, but now it's just a bit much. Ok?" I had sat in silence contemplating the creases on the back of my thumb much like I was doing now. Since that day, my journal had been a chore. I'd kept my entries brief, concise and free of discussion regarding the seam up the back of her stockings. Today, the journal was simple and boring. It didn't take her long to return the notebook to the couch and start the actual discussion with a new question, "What do you want to get out of these sessions?"...

I sat on the exam table in nothing but a pair of jeans and my favorite underwear printed with the furry bust of Chewbacca on the butt. My mother sat in the corner chair, clutching my shirt and coat as if they were the only things left in the world she cared about. She noticed me staring and smiled.

"Are you cold?" she asked.

"No, I'm fine." I looked down at the knees in my jeans. Focusing on the crisscross pattern of threads worn bare by childhood rambunctiousness kept my brain from wondering to darker places.

I looked up as the door opened and my Pediatrician entered. He stopped with an overly dramatic startled look across his face. He stumbled back into the door, mouth agape as if he were facing a lion. In his timid Asian accent, he trembled slightly, "you scared me. I thought I was coming to see a seven year old, not an adult pretending to be a seven year old…" He straightened and placed his hands on his hips. "What's wrong with him, mom?"

"The school nurse called me last week and told me that he'd been caught sleeping at lunch." I turned around on the exam table to look at my mother. This was the first I'd heard about this. I thought I was being careful. She continued, "It wasn't the first time. He's not sleeping at night and I've found him asleep all over the house during the day. When he's caught he acts as if he has no idea he was even asleep. Then, yesterday…"

"Wait," he interrupted my mother mid sentence. "What do

you mean you're not sleeping at night?" he asked. I shrugged and went back to looking for the meaning of life in the worn white spot on my left leg. "Sorry. Continue."

"Then, yesterday I met with his teacher who suggested that he had a bladder infection because he's been going to the bathroom a dozen times each day. I think he's going there to sleep." Her voice broke with the last sentence. "I don't know what to do or how to help him." My mother started to cry silently.

Dr Cheung patted my mother on the shoulder and then took a seat on the exam table next to me. He pulled his stethoscope from his neck to begin his examination with a look of serious concern. Perched beside me, his exam was more awkward than effective. "So what's going on? Talk to me."

"Nothing." I said.

"Deep breathe… and exhale. How's that new baby sister?" He turned to my mother. "Deep breathe… and exhale." He hopped down off the table to grab a wooden popsicle stick from the corner cabinet. "Open and say 'aaahhhhhhh'. Good. Mom, how's he adjusting to not being the only child anymore?"

"He's been wonderful. He's constantly begging to hold her. She cries and he comes running. Why?" she wiped her eyes with a tissue and stood to come over beside me with my shirt.

"There doesn't seem to be anything wrong from my estimation." He patted my thigh and punched at my cheek playfully. He sat down on his stool and rolled over to the cabinet to discard the wooden stick he'd just gagged me with. "I would have to go with my best guess, at this point, call it growing pains and dealing with a new member to the family."

My baby sister had been born only a few weeks prior to my first panic attack. This was the first time it was suggested that my behavior was related to her birth. It would not be the last. After this doctor visit, my family's tolerance turned to discipline.

My parents were now reassured. My pediatrician felt the same as they had, discarding my new sleep routine as a reaction to no longer being the center of attention. A week turned into a month and my routine did not change. As long as I was occupied with something, I was fine. As a mediocre attempt to pass the time, I would watch television until the American Flag test pattern appeared and then read until morning. My parents assumed it would pass, but as it progressed and did not, I found the end of their leniency.

My parents resorted to punishment for my nighttime behavior. I assume that some of you are going to see this as me immediately painting them as the bad guys. I assure you, this is not the case. I don't want you to hold this against them. I've often wondered how I would have handled it as a parent myself. They labeled it behavioral based on my doctor's recommendation. They forbid me from leaving my room at night so the television became off limits. In turn, I resorted to reading. Next they removed my lamp - I found a flashlight. They took the flashlight – I started frequenting the bathroom. And so on. By the end I was left with only the dark and my imagination to drive me to the edge of sanity on the back of a horse named Sleep Deprivation.

Instead of giving up, I fought harder. I wanted to sleep. I explained to my parents that I was going to try to exhaust myself every day, outside, in the heat, in an effort to make falling asleep at night a necessity. It was at this point that my parents decided maybe I wasn't just seeking attention. Their anger turned to sympathy.

CHAPTER 16

A BLINK IN THE DARK

What do I want to get out of these sessions? She'd never before presented me with a question so obligatory. Was she frustrated at my progress? "Why?" I asked. She smiled and stood to lean back against the edge of her desk. "I just want to take a moment and reconsider why it is we're here and what you want to get out of all of this." She gestured around the room with her hands then crossed her arms. Her eyebrows rose to disappear beneath her bangs emphasizing the validity of her quandary. "I want to be able to sleep like a normal kid?" I asked, because I still wasn't sure of the point to this new line of questioning. "You, my dear, are not a 'normal kid' and the one thing I've picked up on in here, spending so much quality time together, is that your lack of sleep bothers everyone else much more so than it does you. I ask again, what do you want to get out of these sessions?" I looked down at a white patch of worn denim on the knee of my jeans. "I want to stop thinking about the universe."...

My insomnia did not get better. The questions in my brain did not go away. Nothing really changed at all; my anxiety only grew worse with each night of personal contemplation followed by a morning full of non-belief on my parents' part.

When my family retreated to their bedrooms and the night took over, without the television or light to read by, I would lie in my bed and immediately go back to the questions that brought on my first panic attack. I would try my best to avoid them, but the more I tried to think about other things, the more my mind raced right back. Where are we? What exactly is the universe and how can it exist without boundaries? What does it all mean? What is life? My chest would start to get tight and the room would begin to spin.

When I was this young, I would let my mind wander and carry my thoughts off to far away places. Sometimes, I would go willingly, other times the destinations it led me to were more frightening than the reality I was trying to escape. The lack of sleep was always more prevalent in the wee hours of the night in my darkened room where the only thing I had to rely on was myself. At the time, I didn't know who to talk to or how to even explain what my mind was going through. I was suffering through each day and barely surviving each night.

Then the hallucinations began.

At first, I wrote it off as my mind playing tricks on me. A shadow would seem to move or shift as soon as I took my eye off of it. The harder I focused on a single spot, the more things seemed to happen around me. You've witnessed it before, the shadow of a coat draped across the chair looks like a man standing in the corner? These instances are nightmares to a child. In my room, the man standing in the corner would move. In my head, he would talk to me.

The first night he came to visit still haunts my dreams.

The rain tickled my window with a lullaby of sand and tin

as the darkness that engulfed the house crept down the hallway and invaded my room. The light from the street lamp shining through my bedroom window was momentarily enraged, flooding the room in a bright explosion of white. My pupils narrowed, leaving the room black once again. Slowly the street lamp beyond began to return to its full luminosity as the hint of a rumble erupted overhead. The thunder built to a crescendo, rolling over the house with such force that my window rattled in its frame. The street lamp, irritated by the flash of light, slowly acclimated back to the dark of night, returning the spilled light to the back wall of my room before the next flash of lightning was able to recycle the process all over again.

My pupils dilated and the shadow behind my dresser came into focus once again. My soccer trophy stretched out along the wood paneling turning a plated plastic bicycle kick into an elongated triceratops holding a zeppelin. I focused my thoughts on the shadow, imagining why a dinosaur would ever need an airship, when the shadow shifted. The triceratops turned its head to look at me. I looked back at the trophy confused and the shadow turned away. My gaze returned to the zeppelin and another shadow grew in the corner near my closet door. I looked directly at the shadow. It looked back. Another flash of lightning and my room was reset.

The shadow returned with the onslaught of my focus. This time, as I stared at the shadow, a face appeared in my doorway, sneaking around the corner of the dark oak frame. I sat up in bed and whipped my head in its direction. Gone. Out of the corner of my peripheral vision appeared another face. I turned my head slowly and it disappeared just the same. The faces would never allow me to see them directly. They were always there and always gone. The shadow creatures watched from just beyond the attention of my eyes. They would hide within the darkness, out of sight but close enough they were not afraid to be seen. Another flash of lightning and my room was reset.

The looming face in the corner stared back at me through black eyes. I ignored the shy faces watching and waiting behind furniture and around corners so that I could peer into the deep black that was The Shadow Man. He blinked and the black was gone. Sheer terror washed over me as the movement took root in my brain. A scream escaped my lungs and pierced the 3am silence. Until this moment my mind was so lost in curiosity that I had rationalized the faces and The Shadow Man as tricks of light. They were more interesting than frightening. Interesting shadows did not blink.

"What's wrong!?" My dad came around the corner and turned on my light, chasing away my audience.

"Nothing. I had a bad dream." I could feel my heart about to explode from my chest as I said the words with calm resolve.

My dad stood in the doorway, his hand on the light switch, trying to figure what to say next. His eyes were closed, trying to bring himself out of his own sleep. "What's wrong?" he asked again, more quietly this time.

"Nothing. I had a bad dream." I repeated more forcefully. I knew attempting to explain any of this to him would be pointless and probably end with me in more trouble than I already was. What would they take away from me next? I'd be sleeping on the floor in the closet if I didn't keep my mouth shut.

He turned the light off without a word, turned on his heel and left my room to return to his own peaceful slumber. I looked back at The Shadow Man and returned to the abyss that rotated malevolently in his eyes. I willed him to blink once again. This time I did not scream.

Putting the pounding of my heart aside I ventured a

whisper, "Who are you?"

The Shadow Man did not move.

"Why are you looking at me?" I whispered.

The Shadow Man did not move.

"Why are you here?" I whispered.

The Shadow Man blinked and goose bumps ran from my wrists to my spine. I pulled the covers tighter and sunk deeper into my pillow. Silence filled my room then gave way to my labored breathing followed by the shock of another distant roll of thunder.

"Who are you?" I whispered again through shaking lips trying to fight back the pending betrayal of another panic attack.

"I am you." The Shadow Man returned with a cheerful whisper. I took a deep breath and held it tight with disbelief. The Shadow Man blinked. The faces all skittered away to the safety of the darkness as The Shadow Man continued in a softer tone. *"I am looking at you because*

you made me." My head filled with black and a panic attack loomed in the recess of my mind. *"Do not be frightened. You bid me to come."* Despite the lilt in his words, I *was* frightened; I did have a panic attack that resulted in me waking up in the kitchen face down on the bench of our breakfast booth.

The next night, The Shadow Man returned. And the next night. And the next. Each time our conversations would find new depth before ending the moment I regressed to self-control. The Shadow Man continued to try to convince me that he was, after all, me.

After a couple of weeks, The Shadow Man left my room and followed me to school. He was quiet and never tried to talk to me, but he did watch intently from the corner, blinking his deep black pits to capture my attention and steal my breath away. When I was at my most vulnerable, he seemed to invade my life.

The more exhausted my brain grew, the more frequent The Shadow Man would appear. Often his arrival coincided with stress. Many times, this stress rode piggyback on puberty. The Shadow Man seemed to delight in my struggles on the sexual front. As I became more in tune with my boyhood fantasies, he almost seemed to push me to act by his mere presence. The suggestion of possibility emanated from his darkness. Some nights he was but a mere whisper in the dark and would bid me to sleep while other nights he would beg me to tell him a story. Some nights he was a black hole in the corner of my room that would ask the questions I couldn't bring myself to consider. *"Where is the end to the farthest reaches of space?"* I would curl in on myself trying to shut him out as he laughed through dead eyes at my despair.

When The Shadow Man ripped open my room to unveil the infinite depth of the universe, sleep would follow as soon as I admitted defeat. The Shadow Man was more than a figment of my imagination. He knew me better than anyone. I did not need to explain my fear to him for he was the embodiment of everything that drove me mad.

CHAPTER 17

CROATOAN

She didn't say a word, simply stood and walked back over to my side. "I think I may be at my end here. Unless you feel like you are still making progress, I can no longer continue these sessions in good conscious without you being aware of what I see as my current limitations. The truth is, I feel like we're spinning our wheels." I looked up then. She was perched on the arm of the couch, looking down at me through pity filled eyes I'd never seen the likes of before. "I do feel like we're making progress. I promise!" I blurted out, pleading now. "I think you are simply getting more used to the situation instead of turning it positive. I'm afraid that if I continue with you, I'm stealing the opportunity from you to grow with another, more capable therapist." I looked at her without the need to manipulate because my honesty ran down my face in swells. "You're giving up on me too."...

After a few weeks I changed my tactics. I resorted to purposely using my vast imagination instead of convoluting my nights with contrived conversations that occurred against my will. If I was able to manipulate the course of the night rather than have the night manipulate me, I felt like I was in control. I would close my eyes tight to avoid the shadows and faces that my mind would convince me were watching me collapse. Instead of contemplating existence, I decided to build a world in my head that I could go to every night. It kept my mind occupied and my nights busy in the comfort of my darkened bedroom.

A full day of running and being as active as possible with the sole purpose of wearing myself out was followed by dinner and a family movie. It was the second day of Christmas break so my thoughts were being split between the questions that plagued me and the need to know what was in each and every present under the tree. More than once I'd tried to develop a worthwhile plan to give me the ability to open up each box, check its contents and return it untouched. The surprise of Christmas had always been my favorite part, but this year I found myself more aggravated at the unknown than excited about the endless possibilities.

My mother sat sideways on the love seat, creating a convenient pocket for me in the corner. I huddled, sitting cross-legged behind the shield her stacked knees created, munching on a bowl of buttered popcorn and homemade fudge. My parents had splurged and bought a Video Cassette Recorder a few weeks prior the same day our tiny town's first video rental store had opened. Movie nights had become a regular occurrence in my house ever since. That night we were enjoying "Popeye" with Robin Williams. I'd already seen the film with my aunt and uncle so my attention found it's way to deeper thoughts.

It had been a while since my first panic attack and I was all but able to avoid them by then. When my mind wandered and the unanswered questions started to monopolize my brain, I was finding new ways to distract myself. Math problems were an easy choice, counting a close second. The defense mechanisms were so prevalent in my thoughts that at times I found myself in the middle of an elaborate quandary about two trains leaving Chicago before I even knew I'd gone there in the first place. That night was no exception.

"Brush your teeth, it's way past bedtime." My dad was already rewinding the VHS tape, standing patiently by the top-loading contraption as the ambient mechanics whirred loudly.

"Did you like it, honey? You didn't seem too impressed." My mother questioned me, aware of my obvious mental drift.

"Oh yeah. It was great, but I remember it from the drive-in. Nothing new." I climbed out from behind my mom-fort and followed my father into the kitchen.

After my bedtime ritual was complete, my dad told me goodnight and my mom lead me to my room. "Are you sleeping any better, baby?" she asked.

"Oh yeah. I'm great. Nothing new." I said as I climbed into bed. I knew there was no point in arguing or attempting to explain the situation to my parents. I'd lost them as allies long ago.

"I worry about you, Travis." She sat down and pulled the covers up to my chin. "*We* worry about you," she corrected.

"I know. I'm fine."

She kissed me goodnight and turned the lights out. I listened for her footsteps as they fled around the corner and down the stairs. My room quickly turned to the nightmare land of The Shadow Man and his many voyeuristic companions. That night I closed my eyes tight and tried to take my mind to a different place than the recent conversations about existence. First, I went back to the Christmas presents. What was in them? What had I asked for? Remembering the box sizes and trying to correlate like requests with sufficient package dimensions ran its course quickly.

If I could have anything in the world, what would it be?

Answers.

Besides answers... anything? Anything in the whole world?

The inconclusive and obvious point of such self-questioning is to occupy the mind. The question worked. I spent the entire night imagining a world where I could have whatever material possessions I wanted. Next came the plot. A back-story followed. Before daybreak I had constructed an entirely new reality in my head.

The dream world consisted of a quarantined town, encased in a glass dome, where only I remained. An alien race had landed on Earth and taken everyone from my city back to the alien's home planet to cultivate him or her for food. I had remained because I was able to hide, being the only one awake at 4:00 in the morning when they had invaded. After their ship had left, the military came in and constructed the giant dome to contain the city because they thought everyone had disappeared because of a special kind of flu that spontaneously combusted the entire population. The town was renamed "Croatoan" for obvious reasons. When I found it safe to come out of hiding, I did so only to be welcomed by an abandoned ghost town. I could go anywhere and do whatever I wanted without consequence. Some nights I'd break into the mall and play video games to my heart's content. Other nights I'd steal cars or even burn buildings to the ground. I could live out my wildest fantasies in Croatoan and no one would ever be the wiser.

Still, the sleepless nights continued without reprieve. Nearly half a year passed before my father asked me to come to the living room for a family discussion. When I arrived my mother was already crying and my father looked concerned.

"What's wrong?" I asked.

"Your mother and I want to know what you need to help fix this." My dad stared at his hands, unable to meet my gaze.

"Fix what?" I asked. Had they found the Playboy I had hidden inside my nightstand or the box of matches in the metal Star Wars lunchbox on my top shelf?

"You're still not sleeping, honey. We're concerned." My mother stood and walked slowly to me. Before she reached me with her outstretched hand, I sat down in the chair and tried to focus on anything other than the tears that stained her cheeks.

"Why now?" I asked. For months, after all of the punishment and betrayal, I couldn't pinpoint the source of their newfound concern.

"Your mother thinks this is getting worse not better." My dad stood and took my mother's hand before she reached me. He spoke in a hushed voice to my mom next. "I am standing firm here. This isn't helping. This is going to make it worse."

"Then, leave me be. I'm his mother and I'm going to do what I think is best." My mom stepped over and took a seat on the armrest of my chair. "Travis, dear, what can I do to help?" Silence took the room by surprise as my dad loomed behind us, waiting for the next opportunity to halt the conversation. "Travis, we'll do whatever you want." My mother offered, which was immediately followed by a huff from my father. I looked up in just enough time to see his back round the dining room table and enter the kitchen.

"I want to be able to sleep and you can't fix that." I stood and walked back up the stairs and into my room. This was my problem; I was going to solve it.

I didn't solve it. The problem persisted. I would spend the next several months petrified of faces in my shadows and figures moving around my room in my sleep deprived hallucination driven bedtime ritual. The only peace came from my nightly excursions into Croatoan. I continued these journeys well into my teenage years. When things were going my way, I'd go a few weeks, even months, without a visit to my domed paradise. When the tables turned and the roller coaster cart crested the top of the hill, it was there, once again welcoming me back as a retreat from the reality that denied me my youth.

CHAPTER 18

STOP TO SMELL THE ROSES

"No, I am not giving up on you." She placed her palm on the top of my head. "I don't want you to ever feel like anyone has given up on you." She ruffled my hair, then quickly removed her hand and walked back over to her chair. She hesitated a moment then turned back toward me. "No matter what happens, Travis, I don't want you to ever think I've given up on you. In all honesty, I've done quite the opposite." I smiled and replied, "Thank you Katherine." She nodded, smiled and turned her back to retrieve some unseen necessity from her purse. The rest of the session we talked about

Atari. She'd purchased a 2600 for her son and was instantly addicted herself. These were the sessions where I left in good spirits. What I wanted most was answers but I was intelligent and self aware enough to recognize my fears as irrational. Seeking answers was not the key and I realized it as such. What I needed was acceptance. I needed someone to believe me. Katherine did just that...

I was already the youngest kid in my third grade class. I'd began school a year early which also made me the smallest. Whenever our class lined up to leave the room for pictures throughout my entire elementary school tenure, I was always at the front of the line, followed by a smattering of petite girls and then the rest of the class. This trend of being the smallest in class remained until I turned fifteen. My height has always been a shortcoming (rim shot?) but not one that I've put much thought behind. That year, I was more than just the young short boy in class; I was also the young short boy who was only in class four days a week.

In the second grade, my teacher had suggested I be tested for early advancement and gifted placement. I was tested yet again and because of a growing interest in education reform under President Reagan, new programs were popping up across the country. Every Thursday I woke up an hour early and was picked up along with a bus full of freshmen and sophomores to be dropped off at our new High School. Along with five other third graders, I attended a special class for advanced study alongside 2,000 teenagers. It was very overwhelming at first, but eventually became the highlight of my educational experience. The program was aptly called "Project Discovery" and continued through the school system for nearly 20 years. My younger sister ended up enrolled in the same program eight years later. It was an honor and a challenge that I do not regret. Many of my teachers did not see it as such. I was often seen as a child being pushed too hard.

What I do regret is all the things I began to miss out on because of this opportunity. Project Discovery opened doors into other advanced placement programs and before I knew it, I was fifteen years old and offered the chance to graduate early. I had only been on a couple of dates and never attended a school dance, prom or a party where anything more than a game of GURPS and a few prank phone calls had been the highlight of the evening. I'd lost my youth. I'd spent it in classrooms, behind desks, in front of a computer, hovered over a piano, working and worrying about everything but what I should have.

I had also been meeting with a therapist. It started out once a month, then grew to once each week. My parents had finally resolved that my sleeping and behavior abnormalities were more than just reactions to an accidental younger sister. Once my gifted schooling began and my parents were approached in regards to my IQ and cognitive scores, their attitude changed. It was suggested that I seek counseling for my issues. I was finally diagnosed as a Chronic Insomniac with Apeirophobia. Giving a name to my problems allowed me to start moving forward instead of being stalled behind something I couldn't explain. I bounced from therapist to therapist for the first year. No one seemed to feel they were able to work with me. At first each felt optimistic, but gradually each, in turn, passed me along to someone else until I met Dr Katherine Hill. She was the light that guided me through my youth. She was also my first crush and ultimately my biggest disappointment.

The sessions with each of my therapists are mostly disjointed memories of smells and furniture. By the time I was ten, the therapy stopped and I spent the next decade trying to forget they ever happened at all. I tried to bleach my mind clean of each and every session. For nearly twenty years I suppressed the memory of ever attending a single session at all. My parents were embarrassed by the debacle and personally I felt as if I was a failure for needing them in the first place. It wasn't until I was in my early thirties that the memories started to return. Slowly they resurfaced. Then more followed, each with greater frequency and intensity.

I sat in my third grade classroom, staring blankly at the chalkboard in front of me. I was listening to the lecture about different animal environments and habitats but was thinking of other more pressing things. I'd read the chapter that morning while eating my Cap'n'Crunch per usual. I didn't want any surprises and everything my teacher was saying was already burned into my brain anyway. Coming to school was a chore. I spent more time teaching myself what was expected at night so that I could draw during class. At first my teachers were always upset with my lack of attention and blasé attitude toward their lectures but by Christmas break I was usually left to my own accord. I was the easy kid for most teachers. The quiet one who never missed an assignment or received less than a perfect score unless the question was wrong or worded incorrectly. They didn't bother me. I didn't bother them.

"Travis, can you answer the next question?" Mrs. Murray asked because she did have to keep up appearances after all.

I looked at my book and searched for the question she was referring to, rewinding the lecture in my brain to search for the last coherent sentence she muttered hoping for a clue to which question we were even on...

"Number three," came whispered over my shoulder by my close friend, Chad.

"Tundra, because of the harsh climate." I returned to my drawing.

"Thank you. Can you please join the rest of the class in turning your book to chapter seven now and answer question three on *that* page."

"Sorry." I put my pad of paper down and flipped ahead a dozen pages to a chorus of snickers. "The food chain shown begins with the sun and ends with the hawk before it recycles itself back through the soil." Then I whispered back over my shoulder through a giggle, "thanks for nothing."

"It's not my fault you're off in la-la land again," Chad muttered low.

The lunch bell rang and everyone began stuffing assignments back into their desk and putting their books away in a frenzied rush. "Travis, can you please see me before you leave?" Mrs. Murray announced over the shuffle of feet and papers. The class let out a low chatter of ooh's and uh-oh's while I made my way to her desk.

As soon as everyone had exited the classroom, I was left standing by her trashcan while Mrs. Murray rooted through a box she had pulled down from an overhead cupboard. "I have something for you," she said. "I think you'll appreciate it."

I was expecting a scolding but instead received a book wrapped in brown craft paper. "Please put that in your bag and don't take it out until you get home. Your mother knows I had intended on giving it to you. Please don't say anything to anyone else, it'll be our little secret." I did as I was directed then hurried off to lunch.

That afternoon, when I returned home, I pulled the wrapped book out of my bag and took it to my mother. "Mrs. Murray gave me this today to give to you."

"I think you misunderstood, dear. This was for you. I already spoke to her about many different things and she thought this might mean something to you. It had meant a lot to her." She handed the book back to me. "Go ahead, open it up."

It was a worn and tattered copy of Herman Melville's "Moby Dick". I'd heard of the novel, but had never attempted to read such a massive piece of literature. "It's huge," I said.

"I read it in school. It was a very hard read, but Mrs. Murray thinks you'll do just fine." My mother seemed pleased.

I spent the next month reading "Moby Dick" whenever I had the chance. At first, it seemed easy to follow and then I found myself reading each chapter twice because I felt like I was missing something. I didn't understand the significance of the novel. Why had she given it to me?

I finished the book, reread it and then returned it to Mrs. Murray before school about two months later. "Thank you," I said, "I really enjoyed it." I sat the book on the corner of her desk and started for my seat at the back of the classroom.

"No, Travis, I want you to have this copy. This was for you.

I read this book several times while I was in college, but it wasn't until I was older that I fully grasped the concept. I hoped it would appeal to you." She handed the book back with a smile. "What did you *really* think of it?"

I hesitated then answered. "It was boring until the last three days. Sorry." I looked down at the book, then back at my teacher. "I felt it was over written like he wanted it to be hard to read. You know, make it seem like more than it is."

"You missed the point entirely." Her face soured. "What did you think of the characters and the story? Not of Melville's literary prowess."

"Why didn't Ahab give up?" I asked. "What drove him to his own destruction? And why would Ishmael stay to witness it all? Why didn't he just jump ship during one of the gams?"

"You're asking questions. I want you to draw conclusions. Wait, better yet, who do you identify with most?"

"Moby Dick." I answered without stopping to think.

"Moby Dick? I meant Ishmael or Ahab… why Moby Dick?" she asked.

"He is the only character in the book who was not given a choice. He was simply running from what hunted him, yet they would not cut him a break. Moby Dick was the good guy. I'd like to think of myself as the good guy."

She stared at me.

"I want you to reread this book again a few years from now. Then again when you are much older. I think each time; it may mean something else to you. For now, I want to offer you this. Sometimes it's important to stop and smell the roses. Don't be in such a hurry to move forward and miss the flowers in front of you." She patted me on my back and sent me to my seat.

I never reread the book.

I continued with Project Discovery until I was in the sixth grade when instead I started enrolling in high school classes. I continued this trend through middle school as well. By the time I reached High School I was already a couple of years farther than my classmates. The homework and studying required to keep up such an educational path was somewhat staggering, but I enjoyed keeping busy. The busier I stayed, the more occupied my mind was and the less time I found myself drifting abroad into darker places.

The busy rush of my childhood did steal away my youth. I'm not complaining because what it did was replace it with something other than fear. For this I have no regret. Whenever I stopped to smell the roses, it gave my brain the time necessary to take me back to the questions and problems that had already taken my youth away long before AP Calculus and Advanced English Lit.

CHAPTER 19

MY CO-PILOT

My sessions continued as expected. Each week we would eat our pre-discussion snack, discuss my sleep for the previous week, check my red journal and finally dig a little into what had happened since we'd last met. Then she decided to ask the hard question. "What frightens you, Travis?" I looked at her, confused, because I was just about to tell her the story of a scuffle that took place in the coatroom the day before over who had the most Star Wars action figures. "What do you mean?" I asked. I knew full well what she meant. I was stalling. "What frightens you? What causes the panic attacks? This is the whole reason we're here after all, isn't it?" I opened my mouth then closed it again. "I thought we were here because I can't sleep." It sounded intelligent. "You're stalling." She was more observant than I had anticipated. I chose to sit quietly rather than answer the question. She chose to observe rather than press. "Yes, we are here because you are not sleeping, but I believe we are both aware of why you are not sleeping. It's the elephant in the room. I think it's time we start to discuss it. Don't you?" I opened my mouth then closed it again before looking down at my faded jeans...

During the summer of my tenth birthday, I became self aware of the conversations that went on within my own head. I don't know any other way to describe it. One day, I was a normal kid (normal with insomnia, apeirophobia and an antagonistic imaginary accomplice known as The Shadow Man... but normal nonetheless). The next day, I had an inner monologue. I think it had always been there, but I was too hyper or too preoccupied to recognize it for what it was.

I had developed a new tactic for combating sleepless nights - sleepovers. No one said a word about a couple of ten year olds spending the entire night playing video games, giggling and eating cold pizza. That summer I spent every single night either at a friend's house or entertaining someone at my own. When I walked around throughout the day, staring out of dead eyes and giving my best zombie impersonation against my will, I was greeted with smiles and jabs in the form of, "Boys will be boys" or "What happened? Stay up all night howling at the moon?" I was running along at a good speed. Things were looking bright. I was on the mend.

"You want to come over tonight?" Mike asked after our normal pre-emptive phone banter had ceased.

"Sure. What do you want me to bring?" I asked.

"Just 'Spider Fighter' and 'Frogger'. Oh and a pillow. Mom's making pizza and Nate's coming too."

The three of us had formed a rotating schedule of overnight arrangements. They had enjoyed the summer as much as myself, but for more adolescent reasons. My ulterior motives were mine and mine alone. Sure, I had a blast with my friends, but it was all a means of distraction. Actually, everything I did was ultimately a means of distraction.

That night, after pizza and a fruitful evening of skateboarding, we found ourselves huddled on the floor in front of Nate's oversized television set. All three of us, earlier that summer, had spent a couple of weeks doing odd jobs and collecting cash to purchase new TV's for our rooms. After watching my dad pick up a 25" television for his bedroom for $30 at a garage sale, I became bound and determined to do the same. Three weeks of picking up trash, trimming bushes, cleaning gutters, mowing grass and collecting aluminum cans had landed us each enough money to find decent floor model color televisions and a handful of Atari games. We were living high on the hog. That night, we were deep into a game of 'Galaga' when Nate's mom made us close the door and turn down the lights. The dark did not frighten me in the company of friends like it did in the solitude of my own room. Knowing what was coming next even guaranteed The Shadow Man would be looking in the corner, but having Mike and Nate with me seemed to squelch my anxiety.

"Time for 'Spice' fellas." Mike rubbed his hands together and made sure his parents had retreated to their own room. We settled in against the end of Mike's bed and waited for him to dial in the forbidden channel we'd accidentally come across while hooking up his parent's discarded cable box. The mythical portal into adult cable porn was lost at the end of static, well off the normal channel guide. As he turned the set top dial to the "U" and turned the secondary knob to 99, we heard the first female moan and subsequent, "just like that, baby."

"Turn it down, turn it down!" Mike urged in a hushed whisper over our uncontrollable giggling.

We snickered and sat in utter awe as our brains frantically tried to make heads or tails out of the wavy green and blue distorted picture. "Is that a boob?" I asked, pointing a finger at the screen.

"I think that's her hair... or a hip?" Nate turned his head to the side and squinted for added effect.

We continued staring at the scrambled signal, laughing at the vulgarity of the crisp audio until, in turn, Mike and Nate finally fell asleep. I left the television on and pretended to watch it until the door opened at 4:00am when in strolled Mike's dad. He stopped, stared at the screen for a moment, stared at our lifeless bodies, laughed and turned off the TV. I continued to keep up the appearance of another sleeping prepubescent boy until he exited and found his way back to his own bedroom.

In the dark of Mike's room that night, under the watchful eye of The Shadow Man, I started to wonder about the depths of space. My mind went back to the questions that have always brought me to the edge of my inner abyss then ruthlessly make me want to jump. I knew if I didn't distract myself, I'd have a panic attack. So far, I'd only had one such mishap in school. All the rest had come in the middle of the night. I did not want to have to explain to my friends or worse yet, their parents, about my anxiety. I tried to breathe. I tried to count. Counting chased away the questions and The Shadow Man as it grounded me to the absolute.

"Two, three, five, seven, eleven, thirteen, seventeen..."

"What are you doing?"

"I'm looking for a way out of this circle," I said.

"It's your choice, ya know."

"That's a shitty thing to say," I retorted. "This isn't helping."

"Sure it is."

"Maybe a little." I stopped. "Why am I talking to myself?"

"You're not. You're talking to me."

"Who is me?" I asked. The Shadow Man had long ago receded into the confines of my mind.

"That's the stupidest question you've ever asked. And you ask a lot of questions."

I sat up and wondered if this was something new or just another part of the sleep deprivation. By now, I'd been accustomed to micronaps, blackouts, The Shadow Man visits and the occasional hallucination so I wasn't too shocked.

"I'm not new. I've always been here."

"What?" I asked.

"You just wondered if this was new? I'm not new. I've always been in here."

"In where?" I was confusing myself.

"In your fucking head. Jesus fucking Christ, it's like talking to a child."

"I am a child," I said.

*"If you think so... You have no idea **what** you are, do you?"*

"I guess not," I answered.

"Stick with me kid, you'll be just fine."

"Do I have a choice?" I asked.

"There is always a choice to be had, you even have the choice to choose it."

"I don't even know what that means," I muttered sarcastically.

"It means, I can be here if you want me to be. I can be gone if you don't. I'll never leave you, but I can leave you be. It's your choice."

"I don't feel like I have many choices. Everything has already been planned and set into motion for me," I said to myself. "This whole life has already happened, I'm just watching it unfold."

"See, I told you that you weren't a child. We're gonna get along juuust fine."

CHAPTER 20

A NEW DIRECTION

My mother pulled up in front of the converted ranch. "I'll be back in an hour." She reached over unlatched my door and kissed me on the cheek in a mock effort to expedite my departure. "I love you," she said as I pushed the massive steel door shut behind me. I strode slowly away from my mom's bright red metallic Lincoln Continental and reluctantly closed the gap between the screen door and myself. I turned the knob without a knock as my routine had been for weeks. The smell of roses was so potent it bordered on toxic. I was forced to take a breath, hold it and then release *through pursed lips. A tire factory going up in flames would have been easier to stomach than this waiting room. My eyes started to water, which could be misconstrued as tears, pissing me off instantly. Stupid flowers. "Hello, Travis. Have a seat, Katherine will be with you in a moment." Normally I would have been excited to see the attractive smile Christie always wore, but lately I was unable to muster even a "hello" in return. I swung my legs freely in the solitary chair while my hands tapped out a beat on the dark stained oak armrests. Once again I found myself staring off into nothing hoping for a piece of space debris to come flying down from the cosmos, crash through the roof and land square on my head...*

My insomnia was in check by the time I reached High School. Well, that's a fully loaded statement. Allow me to elaborate. By the time I turned thirteen, I had my sleeping schedule and daily regimen of exercise and activity down to a choreographed routine. My body functioned well under the constant pressure of school and extra curricular activities. Even when the stress levels peaked, I was able to counteract the symptoms with appropriate preoccupations and distractions. As long as I kept my brain operating, I wasn't allowed to focus on any of my old haunts. Mathematics had become my best friend. The absolute and predetermined nature was calming and soothing. I had found that incorporating mathematics into everything I did allowed me to feel more in control and kept certain aspects of my inner dialogue at bay.

I was still on track for early graduation and was being pressured from all sides to attend an Ivy League school or MIT, if possible. I'd taken the ACT when I was twelve. I'd been drilled and pumped that a 31+ at my age would guarantee admission to wherever I was considering. I had taken the test without practice, under the weight of a head so swollen from ego that my back was sore from holding it afloat by the end of the timed period. I left the testing facility feeling sure I'd at least walked away with a 34 or 35. When the results came in the mail with a resounding "YOU ARE A FAILURE" printed in the center of the certified letter by way of a sad score of 28, my head deflated like a popped balloon. I was grounded back to the reality that I wasn't super human and that things weren't always as easy as those around me pumped them up to be.

I hadn't abandoned my hopes and aspirations for a life of numbers, but I had recommitted myself to my studies. The experience was a humbling one that left me realizing more so than ever, there were limitations to my intelligence. Growing up in a relatively small midwestern city of 50,000 people, it was easy to forget that everything I knew was a drop of water in an ocean of disarray. This was the first time in my life that I began to see the possibility of a future other than the picture that I'd painted many years before. Failure *was* an option.

In the light of this epiphany I was finally finding my way among my peers and starting to fit in as an equal, not as the smart kid who's not supposed to be here and keeps fucking up the curve. I was going out on dates (the girls started to forget that I was a few years younger than everyone else) and found myself within the clique of unpopular, popular kids.

Let's take a minute and peer into the normal subculture that *is* High School. In most academic landscapes, this class structure can be easily divided in the lunchroom. You have the "Jock Table" where all of the most popular athletic students reign supreme. You have the "Popular Table" where the most sought after power couples sit alongside their closest friends and enemies. Often this table can overlap with the previously mentioned "Jock Table"… and the "Support Table", which the cheerleaders and dance squad call home. Next up is the "Band Table".

This table contains the core of the High School Band, in all of their geeky glory. Next up, the "Nerd Table". This group may or may not be involved in band and/or the Audio Visual Club. Seated behind the "Band Table" is the "Goth Table". This is the table throughout the years that's demonstrated raw angst. When I was thirteen, this table included the punks and the most active stoners alike. Standing against the wall next to the trashcans, running in and out of the building to smoke would be the "Hood Table"... sans table. Around the remainder of the lunchroom, the general population made up the "Sheep Tables". Except one, who stood like an island among the mass confusion.

This table, where I found myself residing, was the "Melting Pot Table". The eclectic band of boys and girls could have been placed at any other table, but a common goal of getting out alive rather than fitting into a paradigm prompted this new camaraderie. There were a few punks straddling backwards chairs, a couple jocks took up shop, a band geek and the Valedictorian kept a few more seats warm, a couple token class clowns kept the group lively... and myself. The co-ed group wasn't popular, but everyone knew who they were. They weren't unpopular, but they were never going to be on prom court. I assume every high school had these groups. Being taken in by this one in particular, was the best part of my adolescence. Without this group of friends, I wouldn't have made it through High School as painlessly as I had. Of this group, to this day I'm still very close to more than half. The friends that last a lifetime, blah blah blah, yada yada yada.

"What are you doing?" Stephanie asked. She was the one member of our group that, to this day, I still can't figure out. Gorgeous, funny, charming and popular, yet she chose to surround herself with the likes of this motley crew.

"Drawing. Leave me alone. You're crowding my personal space, woman..." I said, never looking up from my paper.

"What are you drawing?" she asked.

"Would someone get her to shut up?" I asked to no one in particular.

"That's why I love you," she added then curled up against me with obligatory force, before ripping the worn red notebook out from under my hand.

"Fuck Stephanie. You're a tease." I laughed, sitting back in my chair and relishing in the moment of fleeting female affection.

"This isn't a drawing at all. What the hell is this?" She asked.

"It's a script."

"For what?" Nate asked. Although, we were all close, Nate had become my best friend. He was an old soul who was born in the wrong time period. He would have fit in perfect among the greasers of the 1950's, although if asked, he'd have suggested the seventies due to his predilection for vintage punk music.

"A horror movie. Now give it back Steph, or you'll never get to play a part."

She had already started to hand the tattered spiral notebook back but halted and started skimming it again after hearing my last sentence. "Me? You want me in it?"

That started a round robin chorus of "Am I in it?" and "Who am I gonna play?"

"Give me back my notebook. Let me finish the damn thing.

THEN, I'll let you guys see it." I reached over and snatched back the weathered red notebook.

The following two months were saturated with lunch table discussions about the script, suggestions about who was going to play which part and logistical debates over how we would film the more difficult scenes. By spring, I had the entire script completed and was ready to start shooting. I'd saved every penny I made and purchased a decent VHS video camera. Everyone was ready to start as soon as the weather allowed for it.

"Saturday, at my house." I said as I sat down at the lunch table.

"For what?" Chad asked.

"First day of filming," I answered.

The buzz was immediate and intense. The final script centered on a lost girlfriend. The beginning of the film would be the main character searching for her, not knowing what had happened, only knowing that she hadn't been seen or heard from for two days. The story would jump back to the beginning and mention she was obsessed with the dark arts and black magic. It was finally revealed that she had been sucked into an alternate reality of black night when a spell to open a portal between the dimensions failed. The main character travels through the portal, with a rag tag group of friends under the misguided hope of finding her and bringing her back. I hadn't worked out an end under the ruse that it was so awesome I wanted it to be a surprise. In all truth the point of the movie was to have an excuse to get a few friends over to my house all summer, including a few female classmates that I was hoping to get to know on a more intimate level. What started out as a joke had quickly evolved into a major undertaking.

The first Saturday, the only things completed were the establishment of characters, the devouring of three-dozen chocolate chip cookies and a full day of hanging out with my best friends. The video camera was never even removed from its pleather duffel. All in all, it was a complete success. The next week, much of the same. By the third week however, I knew we had to move forward or everyone would lose interest.

My close confidant, Mike, would play the main character. The brooding hero was no stretch at all. Stephanie would play the role of the lost girlfriend. Nate would play the demon spirit holding Stephanie hostage and manipulating events from beyond the portal. The rest of our troop filled in both in front and behind the camera. I relinquished video duties to Chad and played the role of director. After all, it was my house, my camera, my script and my vision.

During the middle of the summer, the weekend project became a full time job. What began as Saturday afternoons hanging out at my house became five days a week, on location and every night at someone's house, editing footage between two parallel VCR's. I was becoming obsessed with completing the movie under illusions of grandeur that the final piece would somehow give my life new direction. When you're thirteen, every day is the beginning and end of a life experience. With my masterpiece I was going to change the world.

The last three weeks of summer, I needed to cut filming short in order to study for the ACT. I was scheduled to retake the test the week before school resumed. I'd spent the entire summer trying to forget my last botched attempt. Now, with a new date bearing down, the stress was again renewed. Trying to divide my time between the two endeavors was beginning to take its toll.

"You need to kill the movie and focus on what's important... the test," I said.

"What if the movie is a means to an end?"

"An end to what?" I asked

"An end to everything. Can't you see the possibilities of what you're doing?"

"I need to do well on the test. The movie is insignificant." I ignored the nagging voice.

"You need to stop worrying about the test and focus on the movie, but we need to make changes. The movie can be something great. Something fantastic. You need to listen to me."

"You make no sense. The test is most important. If I have any intention of pursuing math, physics or quantum studies, I need this test score. It's paramount." I resolved to ignore my own inner monologue.

Each day I studied. I took practice test after practice test and commissioned my mother to field my friend's requests to take time away from the task at hand. I basically shut myself in my room and focused on the ACT.

All the while, the argument continued.

"You need to change the movie. I have a vision, hear me out."

Finally, I gave in to the persistent voice. "What's the change?"

"The demon holding the girlfriend needs to be holding her for the sole purpose of sucking Mike into a timeless state. The demon kills Stephanie in front of Mike... no wait, better yet, she SACRIFICES herself in front of Mike. This betrayal and pointless journey drives him mad and he returns to the beginning of his quest via a magical spell, hell bent on doing it all again in an infinite loop. He wants to feel the pain over and over again, punishing himself for his failure. The infinite loop of pain and loss drives him mad and you never know if he's nuts because of the loop or if he creates the infinite loop because he's nuts."

"I think *I'm* nuts." I went back to the P-ACT in front of me.

"Why would you think that?"

"Because I'm arguing with myself over a film so far beyond

the talent and ability of what I have to work with. This is nothing more than me trying to distract myself from failing the ACT again."

"A 28 was not failing," Silence… my brain already back in the midst of the deep concentration required for a practice test.

The following two weeks, the stress grew to an all time high. I ended up in the hospital with a bleeding ulcer two days before the test. A nervous breakdown the week after the test in front of Nate and Mike while we were editing footage, complete with a full-blown panic attack and temper tantrum highlighted the last few days before school started.

I never changed the movie. We finished as it was originally written. My internal argument subsided when we finally showed the movie to our school's youth group. I was disgusted with the quality of the final project, all my newfound desires for a life outside of math went up in smoke when I was forced to watch the final cut in front of a house full of fifty kids from my school. I wanted to vomit as my stomach twisted under the visual evidence that a camcorder from Sears and a group of friends created realistic limitations that collided head on into my artistic intention.

Everyone who saw the forty minute finished product disagreed. By Thanksgiving, I couldn't walk from class to class without being asked for a copy in the halls. At first I refused out of embarrassment. Eventually the requests stopped. Nate and Mike were making copies in my stead, meeting the demand of our school.

Nate and Mike never mentioned to anyone the night at my parents house when a fit of rage ended with a broken mirror, a fist through my bathroom door and me passed out on the floor in my mother's arms after I was unable to slow my breathing and the panic attack stole me away from consciousness.

Later that year, I was sitting in AP English Lit when my art teacher entered the room and approached me on bending knee. "Travis, can I kidnap you for a few moments? There's someone I want you to meet." She excused me from class and took me to the guidance counselor's office. Waiting there was a man in a pair of weathered jeans and a red button up shirt. He didn't look a day over thirty and appeared to be straight out of a music video with his earrings and a sleeved tattoo creeping down the back of his hand from the unbuttoned cuff on his right arm.

"I'm Scott, you must be Travis." He reached out to shake my hand.

"Yeah?" I had no idea what was going on.

"Mrs. Heath sent me a copy of your movie. I have to say that I'm a little jealous." He laughed and turned to Mr. Pratt, my guidance counselor. "You didn't tell me he was so young!" Scott turned back to me and scooted to the edge of his chair. "Please tell me you want to do this when you grow up."

I looked around, completely confused. "Do what?" I asked.

"*Do what*, he says." Scott sat back and crossed his arms in a fit of mock disgust. "Make movies, of course!"

"Scott is from the University of Cincinnati. He works in the Industrial Design program there. Do you know what Industrial Design is?" Mrs. Heath, my art teacher, asked. I shook my head.

"Industrial Design," interrupted Scott, "is the..." He thought for a minute running his hand through his trimmed goatee. "Ok, imagine this. You get up on Saturday and head to the movies. You watch a great flick about aliens and the war for survival on a distant planet. An Industrial Designer did that." He smiled, waiting for my reaction. I gave none, still confused. "An Industrial Designer created the aliens, made the special effects, helped produce the movie, made the logo, came up with the tagline, designed the posters in the lobby. Hell, he designed the lobby... the whole damn theater! He mapped out the parking lot and worked as the city planner to develop the entire complex. He even designed every one of the damn cars filling the fucking parking lot!" He paused, looked around and offered an apology for his over enthusiastic colorful performance before returning to his speech with a more subdued tone. "The Industrial Designer can do all of that. With that knowledge and skill set, he can also write the movie and direct it on top. Now, how does that sound?"

I turned to Mrs. Heath, "Why am I here?"

Scott laughed, Mr. Pratt sighed and Mrs. Heath explained. "We think you would do really well at the University in the Industrial Design program. I know you're dead set on MIT, but I think you'd be happier creating things. You are incredibly talented. I don't want to see you squander that."

"An art school would be squandering his academic

achievements." Mr. Pratt leaned on his desk, obviously frustrated. "I have your ACT results here. Would you like to take them home to open with your parents, or would you like to see how you did now?"

I looked down at the envelope and nearly threw up that day's tacos all over his oversized desktop calendar. "No, I think I'll take it home to my parents." I reached out and took the envelope.

"Walk with me," Scott said as he stood and grabbed me by the shoulder, dragging me to my feet. Once I was on solid footing he patted my back and walked me through the office door and beyond into the hallway. "You're a young kid with a bright future. Do you like Star Wars?"

"Sure, who doesn't?" I offered.

"Exactly. That's my man. I worked on 'Jedi' at Industrial Light and Magic. It was the crowning achievement of my young adult life. I got very little credit and no money for my efforts, but I was part of the team. That's all that mattered to me. I was told that you already have a 28 on your ACT, why the hell are you taking it again?" He didn't offer me the time to answer, but instead continued talking without skipping a beat. "With a 28, you're already accepted in

Cincinnati. With your current portfolio... you have a portfolio right? With your work and this video tape," he tapped a black VHS tape against the palm of his hand, "I can guarantee you entrance into the program. Think about it. You'll go farther here," again, he pointed at the videotape, "than there." He tapped the ACT results in my hand.

We stood in the hallway, the silence between us satiating the awkwardness.

"You don't talk much," Scott chuckled. "A lot going on up there I bet." He rapped his fist on the top of my head gently then smacked me in the chest as he walked backwards down the hall in retreat. "I'll see you in the studio. I know you'll make the right decision." Scott turned and waved a tattooed hand bedazzled with silver rings over his shoulder as he jogged toward the exit.

That night, I mulled over the decision while the ACT score sat dormant in my backpack.

"I think Design would be therapeutic," I offered, to get the argument started.

"Mathematics can be therapeutic and maybe even provide

an answer or two," I countered myself.

"Are you willing to give up a chance to create amazing things for the small hope that a lifetime of obsession and devotion could somehow resolve your fears through the discovery of something you have no idea whether or not it exists, is possible, or is even discoverable within this lifetime? Or the next hundred lifetimes for that matter?"

"So, everything I've worked for has been pointless? I'm going to give up all my hard work and continued devotion to my studies to... what? Draw pictures?" The thought of giving up on math made me nauseous.

"Who said you would be giving up? Maybe this is what you were destined to do all along? Ever think about that?"

"I don't believe in fate. I make my own decisions." I huffed.

"You're naïve. You've already decided this decision; you're trying to convince yourself. Just shut the fuck up, take a breath and do what you feel like fits."

I registered at the University of Cincinnati for the Industrial Design program by the end of the year, abandoned my hopes at quantum mechanics and changed my whole life direction based on a whimsical ploy aimed at getting a few girls over to my house, the influence of a fast talker and the transparent words of my inner co-pilot.

My ACT score was a 32.

CHAPTER 21

FIRST LOSS

"Travis?" The door opened and I was ushered back down the familiar hall to Katherine's office where she stood waiting in the doorway. "Where's your sleep journal?" she asked as I slipped by under her arm. She'd obviously noticed my empty hands. "It's gone." I took the same seat I'd taken for as long as I could remember. "What do you mean it's gone?" She asked, closing the door behind her. "Gone. Just gone." I said, not wanting to admit that I had burned it on the garage floor three nights prior in a sleep deprived haze. Somehow I had convinced myself that the red

spiral notebook was a magical device that needed to be destroyed in order for my body to find the rest it needed. In those moments, when my heart rate peaked and the sweat beaded on my forehead, my body chose fight over flight. It wasn't until the next morning that I had to decipher what I had done and what I had to do to cover it up or face the consequences. There was no point in trying to forge a replacement journal. What was done was done. My best bet now was to change the subject, "So... peanut butter sandwiches?"...

The following spring break, right before I was set to graduate High School and head to the University of Cincinnati, I woke up Monday morning and immediately felt like something was wrong. I know this may sound contrived, but bear with me. It was raining and the air felt heavy. I got out of bed and shut my window, wiped up the puddles on my desk and headed to the bathroom. By the time the toilet had finished refilling from the last flush, the phone rang. I didn't want to answer it so I stayed in the bathroom, hiding.

Fucker would not stop ringing... I made the decision to see who it was rather than wake up the rest of the house. As soon as I reached the receiver, the incessant ringing ceased. I turned and headed back toward the bathroom before it started up again. "This better be good."

"What is it?" I answered the phone in my morning voice.

"Uh, it's Chad, did you hear what happened?"

Our gang still skated together, got into trouble and rented movies. Out of that group, five of us were still really close: Mike was our fearless leader; Eric was our very own Casanova (the only one of us with a girlfriend at the time); Chad had the basement where we usually corralled; I was the instigator; and Nate was the free spirit, my best friend. "No... what happened?" I replied, still trying to open my eyes all the way and join the world of the living.

"Um, we think Nate... Uh, well Mike and I heard Nate died last night." There was something in Chad's tone that was all too unsettling. It wasn't funny.

"Seriously? Where did you hear that? No way, he just called here last night, but I wasn't home. He probably started the rumor himself," I sputtered back, laughing at the thought of Nate's departure. I was wide-awake at this point.

"Fuck you, I'm just telling you what we heard. Mike just left and said he tried to call his house but no one answered. He called Kentucky Fried Chicken, thinking Nate was at work." Chad was speaking so fast, I could hardly take it all in. "They said something like, 'Sorry, but Nathan committed suicide yesterday'." Chad acted as if I had called him a liar and spit in his face through the receiver.

"Suicide? Bullshit! I'll call you back!" I slammed the phone and found myself shaking. I didn't want to believe it, but there was something in Chad's voice, a subtle disbelief on his part. I know now that he was probably in shock. As much as I didn't want to believe it, I knew deep down, in that moment, it was true. It was confirmed after I called the KFC where Nate worked, and was met with the same response Mike and Chad had already received. I hung up the phone and stood there. My mom had gotten out of bed from the nonstop ringing of the phone and was now making her way to the kitchen.

"What's wrong? What happened?" she asked in her best upset-mom voice. Her eyes looked so innocent when she spoke. She had no idea. How could I tell her? There was nothing to tell, and everything to say. I just stood there for what felt like hours, looking at her, searching for an answer.

"Nate committed suicide," I whispered, still pondering the reality of it in my head. Better to just rip the band-aid off quickly... My mom looked into my eyes and started to cry. Her tears fueled rage; I wanted to wreak destruction on the world. I needed release. I wanted to destroy something, direct the pain outward.

"Why?" I asked my co-pilot. My heart wanted to weep, but my head wanted to scream with rage.

"He found a way out."

"Fuck you." I hated the thought.

"He always finds a way out."

Eric came over and picked me up later that day. He wanted to do something, anything, to keep us occupied. We ended up at Chad's and kind of sat around afraid to say anything. The tension in the air was choking us dry. The group was there because we had to be together. We were all afraid to be alone. Eric decided to call Mike at home, but his Dad ran interference on the phone. Eric looked worried when he hung up.

"I think we should go talk to him," Eric decided calmly.

I couldn't understand how he could appear so detached. For me speech had ceased all together. I wanted to say so much and had no idea how. Chad and I sank into Eric's car and headed toward Mike's house while Eric stayed behind and manned the phone. After a few minutes of guzzling gas, Eric's 1971 Cougar spit us out in front of Mike's house. After trying to secure passage to Mike's upstairs bedroom without success, his mom finally circumvented his father and went up to get him for us.

A few minutes later she came back down looking confused. "He's not up there." She turned around and walked back into the heart of the house, leaving us in the foyer by ourselves.

It didn't take us long to track him down. "There he is..." I pointed across the Library parking lot at the church courtyard. Mike stood by himself in the middle of the concrete, bouncing a basketball and taking free throws. We snaked our way through the alley and parking lot to come to a stop behind where he continued to take potshots at the chained rim.

"Mike, how long you been here?" Chad asked. Mike

offered no response.

"Dude, come back to Chad's with us." I walked over next to him so I could see his face. Mike, again, offered no response.

"What the fuck? Say something." Chad took a step forward and grabbed the ball on its last bounce before it reached Mike's outstretched hands. We all stood in silence.

"Fuck this." Chad dropped the ball at Mike's feet and walked past him to the still running Cougar. "Are you coming?"

I stood in front of Mike for a minute longer. "We need you. We'll be at Chad's house." I walked by, and patted him on the shoulder. He looked through me and finally bent to retrieve the basketball as I got into the passenger side of the Cougar.

The rest of the week was sort of a blur. I didn't go to work at all. I slept at Chad's house the first couple of nights. Unfortunately, my parents left for Las Vegas that week for an anniversary getaway with another couple. I started at Chad's house, but ended up floating from friend's couch to friend's basement to my cousin's bedroom floor. The funeral was the following weekend. The services were mass confusion highlighted with blood, tears, hate and regret. We were young and stupid, looking for a way to vent.

Vent I did. That night started out with two (not one, but two) McPizzas. If you're not old enough or privy, McDonald's actually had Pizza in the early ninety's. It was terrible and cheap. The pizzas somehow ended in my first (and only) experience with alcohol during my short tenure at High School.

The next morning I woke up at the wheel of my cousin's 1985 Monte Carlo. The front bumper securely lodged into the side of an enclosed front porch attached to an empty house behind the levy near the local power plant. The car wouldn't start (we later discovered it had ran out of gas) so I abandoned it and started walking to Chad's house.

By the time school reconvened, Nate had already been forgotten. No tree was planted in his memory. No plaque was hung in the lobby. No moment of silence. No Nate.

"Why?" I asked my co-pilot. My heart wanted to weep, but my head wanted to scream with rage.

"He found a way out."

"Fuck you." I hated the thought.

"He always finds a way out."

CHAPTER 22

THE FRESHMEN FIFTEEN

"No sandwiches today, I'm afraid. Today, we bite the bullet and start talking about your fears." She walked over to her desk, grabbed her chair and wheeled it around to face me on the couch. She picked up one end of the coffee table and pivoted it 90° to give her an unobstructed view. Moving the giant red coffee table also blocked my exit. I was trapped. Five minutes passed in silence. I looked down at the knees of my jeans. Focusing on the crisscross pattern of threads worn bare by childhood rambunctiousness kept my brain in brighter places. "If you're not ready to talk about

any of this, we can just sit here. I'm not opposed to it." Five minutes more passed in silence. "I really think getting it out of your head is going to do more good than you can imagine." Five more minutes passed in silence. "Do you know what your fear is called?" she asked. I ventured an upward glance in her direction. "It's called Apeirophobia. It's the fear of infinite things. Did you know it was called that?" Five minutes more passed in silence. "It's really more common than you think..." she said. "How do you fix it?" I interrupted...

I started college while I was still in High School. I didn't have the luxury of a driver's license or the ability to crash in a dorm. I rode to school each day with friends, then walked a half mile along the track team's cross country trail that snaked through the woods separating my High School from the area college. My classes consisted of the highest-level mathematics and physics courses offered in the local curriculum as well as a smattering of psychology and fine arts to keep me sane. Nothing on my schedule required a massive amount of thought or effort, but it was still more challenging than High School had been.

The first day of class, I wasn't worried. I wasn't nervous. If anything, I felt calm and at ease. A feeling of déjà vu washed over me as we walked through the giant automatic doors into the Psychology Building. I stood beside the water fountain and watched students of all ages walk by carrying backpacks and books. Everyone seemed so tall and oblivious. Each person was headed off in his or her own direction, intent on solving a problem or meeting a deadline. The looks on each of their faces made me feel small and insignificant. I took a deep breath and made my way to my first class.

Immediately I felt like I was seen as the creepy little kid in the front of the classroom. I'd finally become accustomed to standing out in the High School setting, looking more like a small freshman than a child among adults. The college classroom was a giant leap backwards on the physical progress I'd made among my peers. The difference between state college and High School wasn't the classes or the curriculum as much as it was the average students attending. My classes were full of the newly graduated, looking for an excuse to keep mom and dad off of their back by signing up for a few classes *or* the middle aged adult trying to get back into the swing of school in order to find a way out of a dead end job that ended each transaction with, "thank you and have a nice day." Regardless of the students on either side of me, I was not met with ridicule as I was in High School. Instead I was met with admiration and awe.

"You're a little kid. Are you some kind of freak?" was replaced with, "That's amazing! How old are you again?"

Being the only student my age the first year the city offered this advanced placement; I stood out among the collegians. I was often stopped on my way to class and asked questions by housewives confused by their math homework or fought over in lecture when dividing up for group projects. I'd gone from the curve wrecker to the helpful wiz kid by a simple trek through some trees and over a log or two.

My fifteen minutes lasted just that.

My second year attending class, an influx of High School students flooded the hallway. Based on our positive reception, the school board approved nearly a dozen more seniors the following year. Although they were all still much older than me, the novelty of my youth had long since worn off. What was once new and exciting quickly became another addition to the daily routine. It had been nice standing out in a positive way for a change. It was then that I decided to go ahead and graduate early, walk with the senior class and take up the standing offer to attend the College of Industrial Design in Cincinnati.

When I was seventeen, I moved a hundred miles from home and bunked with one of my best friends from High School. At seventeen, I was still under curfew age, but my physical appearance had finally met up with my intelligence. I no longer looked out of place. As long as my driver's license stayed in my wallet, I fit right in.

At first, things went really well. The University was not much different than college back home. I was able to keep my life busy with a handful of electives including racquetball and rock climbing. I was meeting new people and spent nearly every waking hour with the girl I'd brought along from home. Technically she was a year my senior, but based on maturity, no one complained. I was fast tracking into my college through the foundations base per my meeting with Scott. My parents had taken me to the school over the summer for orientation and met with the Dean where the fast track plan was also confirmed. I'd already attended all of the entry-level art classes over the summer at my home college so everything was review on top of it all. My credits would not transfer, but I considered the last three months practice for the real thing. Everything was right with the world.

Until Christmas break.

Right before the University closed for the holiday, the director of our foundations program pulled each student aside to discuss his or her progress. I expected, "You're on target, we'll see you in Industrial Design come next fall." Instead I was smacked in the face with, "I assume you'll have a full portfolio together by the time you return from break?"

"What's the purpose of the portfolio?" I asked.

"The evaluation for the Industrial Design program will be the second Wednesday in January. We're only offering forty spots. Right now, two hundred of you were accepted to foundations. One hundred and sixty people will have to reapply to foundations or switch majors."

"But, wait, what? I was already accepted. I have my letter and everything." I argued nervously.

"Hold on, let me check my paperwork." I waited while the director consulted his legal pad, flipped through notes and finally pulled out an official letter. "Ok, here it is." He spun the letter around, directing it at me. "This was sent to your home address three weeks ago. Based on the recommendation of our new Dean, we are no longer fast tracking recruited students into the program without a portfolio review. You'll have to fight for your spot the same way everyone else does. No free rides here." He started to pull the letter back, but I snatched it away before his hand was halfway there. Scanning the letter I confirmed the director's summation. "Here is your copy of the portfolio requirements. You should be fine, just make sure you come back from break fully prepared." He pulled the letter out of my hand and replaced it with a packet of black and white copies prominently labeled "PORTFOLIO REQUIREMENTS".

I left the meeting in numb shock.

"What the fuck am I going to do?" I asked.

"You're gonna suck it up, grow a set and make this shit happen."

"What if I don't get in?" I asked.

"You'll get in. I'm sure of it. You've been here and done this all before. You always come through. You've never failed yet. You'll be fine."

"I wish I had your confidence," I mused.

"You do. This is your confidence."

I decided it would be better for me to stay in the dorm and work twenty-four hours a day over break to ensure I had a stellar portfolio rather than going home and dealing with the distractions of the first Christmas after flight from the nest. Insomnia had long since become my best friend. If I was careful to keep stress levels in check, my body ran like a well-oiled machine.

My stress was not in check.

I returned home the morning of Christmas Eve with several facial ticks, a returning ulcer, a slight stutter when I got overly nervous and a mind that couldn't keep from running off to questions about the boundless reaches of the universe. The more potent the stress, the more frequent and violent my panic attacks.

The drive home from the University should have lasted ninety minutes, but ended up taking nearly four hours. I had to get off at every other exit for food and drinks just to keep my mind focused on the road. Twenty miles from home, I pulled over and called my Grandfather from a pay phone to come get me. I used a broken down car as my excuse. I hung up the receiver, popped my hood and loosened my positive battery terminal. By the time my Grandfather arrived, I was fast asleep in the back seat of my Chevelle.

It took me the next three days to wake back up enough to know exactly where I was and what was going on. Christmas was a blur, peppered with blackouts and forgotten conversations. Somewhere in there, I asked my girlfriend to marry me. The decision had been made years before I had ever met her.

"What are you going to get her for Christmas?"

"I don't know. I haven't thought about it, I've been so busy. Thoughts?" I asked my co-pilot.

"It's time to ask her to marry you."

"It's too soon." I quickly replied, but then rethought the decision. "Is it too soon?"

"No. This is the course you've always planned."

"No it isn't. I've always wanted to spend my days in the mountains of Montana, a recluse, working out the mysteries of dark matter and subatomic particles in my private lab, hell-bent on finding the answer to the question, 'where does the universe end?' Not popping out two and a half kids plus a dog behind a white picket fence." I scoffed at the notion.

"I've always known you were going to get engaged your freshmen year. Stop thinking with your brain. You know it just feels natural. Search your heart."

"Technically it's not my freshmen year," I clutched at straws.

"Technically, you've already decided to ask her to marry you, you're just trying to convince yourself."

CHAPTER 23

NEXT COMES MARRIAGE

"We talk about it first. That won't fix it, but it will bring the real problem to the surface." She stared hard at my face, searching for her own answers. "Do you believe in God?" she asked after a moment's hesitation. I tilted my head and replied, "Do you?" She sat for a moment, and then answered honestly, "Yes, I believe I do. There has to be a greater power than us. That's just how I feel. It doesn't make it the correct answer but it does make it my answer." I looked back down at my jeans; "There's no point to any of this then." She could hear the defeat in my voice and *immediately replied, "Why would you say that, Travis?" I looked back up into her face, "If you believe in God, you can't begin to understand what it is I go through. When you look into the night sky, you already have the answer. Albeit an irrational and stupid answer based on myth and outdated folklore, but an answer in every other connotation of the definition. It isn't the correct answer, but it does make it your answer."...*

Immediately following the engagement, the wedding plans went into full force. Flowers, guest lists, venues, churches, vows, colors, tuxes and dresses. I avoided it all like the cancer that it was. You want to create Elizabethan drama complete with backstabbing, mystery, intrigue, heartache, lost friendships, sleepless nights and an overabundance of tears... forget daytime drama; *plan a wedding.*

I wanted nothing to do with it. This was part of the plan to get me to my life goal that my co-pilot reminded me at every turn was an integral part of the American dream. Forget the fact that when I purchased the ring, I was still bound by a state mandated curfew of 11:30. It was already planned out and in motion long before I walked into the jewelry store.

*"Stop thinking about it. Look into your heart. You know this just feels right. It feels like you've done it before. It just feels **right**. Admit it."*

"If I get married, I'm going to be stuck here. I'm going to have to give up my dreams in exchange for security. Am I willing to do that?" I asked.

"Yes, you are. Besides, what dreams are you referring to that marriage is going to interfere with? This is the right course. This is the expected course. Search your heart and you'll realize that I'm right."

"Can I have some of your confidence here?" I pleaded.

"I who have nothing. I who have no one."

"What the hell does that mean?" Confused, I lost myself in my own distracted thoughts.

"I'm just a no one with nothing to give you."

"What?" I asked.

"Confidence. I have none. I'm simply stating the facts. I'm

here to guide you down the path that's already planned. I'm the voice of reason that keeps you aimed like an arrow on your target. When you stray, I kick you back on course."

"I'm not straying. I'm considering all my options." I say with little conviction.

"You haven't had any options for eons. This is just cold feet. Get over it."

"I hate when you get all dreary and dark," I muttered to myself, knowing full well he could hear me even when the conversation was outside the confines of my own private hell.

"WE get all dreary and dark. Don't forget, we're in this together. I don't want to be here anymore than you do."

I listened to my co-pilot's advice. I started out in the maternity ward nursery with a group of like newborns. When they were coloring pictures of houses, I was reading Moby Dick. When they were enjoying their first kiss, I was meeting with college recruiters. When they were pinning the corsage onto their prom date, I was getting engaged. When they were considering a major, I was walking the aisle.

"Was this a good decision?" I asked.

"This wasn't a decision, good or bad. This was destiny. Seriously, when is this going to sink in?"

"I don't like feeling as if my choices have already been made," I looked down at my wedding ring. "This isn't the life I expected."

"This is the life that you have. What we expect and what we have are two different things. Are you happy? Do you love her?"

"I want a house in the mountains, overlooking a valley where I can eat my breakfast on the deck and watch the elk graze as I crunch my corn flakes."

"In the next life. Maybe. For now, stay the course. Also, you didn't answer the questions. Are you happy? Do you love her?"

"Fine. I'm happy. Yes, I love her. I always have. It does feel... *right.* Besides, I hate corn flakes."

"Exactly."

"Déjà vu?"

"Exactly."

PART III

ROCK BOTTOM

CHAPTER 24

OFF TO WORK

"You think that my beliefs in God keep me from having an objective outlook on your fears?" Katherine asked, obviously taken aback by my inference. "Yes, in a nutshell." I said as a matter of fact. "We're discussing your beliefs not my own," she rescinded. "No, what I'm saying is that if you have the ability to close off your mind and accept ridiculous notions like God and the Bible, then you're not intelligent enough to see the forest for the trees." I was getting irritated. "Had I known you were this stupid, we could have saved a lot of peanut butter sandwiches and I could have been

spending my Wednesday afternoons at home playing Pitfall. The next thing you'll tell me is that you believe in time travel too," I said. "Why would you ever associate a belief in God with time travel? Please explain," Katherine continued. "Both are ridiculous fantasies because if it were to ever be possible, at any point in the future, somehow, somewhere, somewhen, someone would have traveled back in time to say hello and brag about their time machine. The only plausible explanation is that a) it is science fiction and will never be possible or b) the world ends before it is invented." "That doesn't answer why you would associate time travel with a belief in God," she pointed out. I stood from the couch and climbed over the coffee table. "Don't get up, I'll show myself out." Katherine watched as I walked to the door and opened it. I hesitated for a moment trying to decide whether it was a good idea to slam it behind me or leave it open. She never moved from her chair as I strode back down the hall toward the waiting room, the door wide open behind me...

A full time job was already waiting for me by the time I graduated from college. I'd been hired two years prior, while I was still in my undergrad program. Within a month I was promoted to Director of Design. It was neither what I wanted to do nor where I wanted to be, but the pay was respectable, the people worth interacting with and the work rewarding. I still harbored plans for greater things, but I set them aside and spent everyday making sure each and every thing I touched was completed with care and precision. My output reflected my attention to detail and drive for success. I was young, ambitious and knew everything there was to know about the professional world.

New-Graduate-Itis.

With new responsibilities came new problems. With new problems came old issues. I'd spent the last few years suppressing, successfully, everything that kept me awake at night. Keeping busy and focusing all of my attention on the immediate future had given me the distraction necessary to sit on the porch of our new house after dark in peaceful silence. I could even sneak a peek at the stars overhead every now and again without fear of waking up facedown on the deck boards hours later. I hadn't had a panic attack in years. I was able to get in bed at night, close my eyes and rest. Even if I wasn't able to sleep, I could at least take a jaunt down Main Street in Croatoan or sit up against the wall and bring a Rubik's Cube to multiple climaxes until my mind shut down or the sun came back up.

With new responsibilities came new problems. I had been hired as a Director, but I was actually working as a Product Manager. Not only was I dealing with design but also fighting with manufacturing and retail inventory. Spreadsheets and numbers were prevalent so I was a natural at first. Throw in human error coupled with minimum wage retail associates... my overwhelming desire for perfection hit a brick wall. For the first time in my life I was unable to ensure the perfect outcome of each and every project I touched. I'd never been dependent on someone else in order to complete a task.

I'm not a team player. I've never been a team player. I will probably never be a team player. All through college, this had not been a factor. In the real world where you're completing projects in turn for a paycheck, everything is a team effort. My quality and production levels were top notch... my people skills were lackluster at best.

The problem stemmed from this newfound arena of dependency. Directing someone else and then waiting for them to complete something I could do myself in half the time drove me insane. It wasn't long before I was working seventy to eighty hours each week over a full staff only working thirty to forty because I was sending them home early. I would have rather had an empty department to get everything done myself than waste half my day explaining how and what to do to each of them.

"Scoot over for just a second," I said. Repeat. Repeat. Repeat.

I spent more time correcting and attending to other designers' projects than I ever did my own. I felt like a kindergarten teacher. I was a terrible boss. I was a controlling designer. I was driving myself to an early grave.

CHAPTER 25

SUCKING OUT THE INFECTION

My mother was not near as excited at my early dismissal from therapy as I had expected her to be. "You are going to march right back in there and apologize to Katherine. Then you're gonna sit your happy ass down and listen to what she has to say." My mother: the pragmatist. "But mom, she doesn't talk. She just listens. I talk to myself all. The. Time. This is just a waste of your money." I pleaded the financial angle knowing my mother's partiality toward the pinched penny. "Don't make me drag you back in there kicking and screaming because, trust me, I will." My mother: the disciplinarian. I went back inside, never said a word to Christie and simply walked back down the hallway. I waited outside her door for nearly a full minute before I knocked...

"Wake up."

"I am awake," I said.

"No you're not. Wake up."

"Fuck. I said I was awake," I bit back.

"Oh yeah? Do you see that guardrail?"

Stress from the new venture into the world of corporate America drove me to the brink of self-destruction while I drove my pickup truck into a guardrail at 7:30 am on the way to the office after a three-day bender surviving on nothing more than caffeine and late night video games. The entire passenger side of my Chevy S-10 was destroyed in an instant as I started to nod off and pulled the wheel to the right. I walked away from the accident with only a couple bleeding knuckles from the steering wheel and a sore neck from being tossed side to side. I finished the commute into work and then called the insurance company.

"Hello, State Farm Insurance, this is Kathy," the friendly neighborhood voice greeted me.

"Hi Kathy, it's Travis. Unfortunately, I wrecked the truck again."

"Again? Travis, you need to be more careful. What happened this time?" she asked.

"You'll never believe this. I was on my way to work this morning and went into a sneezing fit. Somehow I ended up against the guardrail." I chuckled to emphasize the ridiculous nature of the incident.

"That's horrible. Let me consult your policy and see what I can do."

It wasn't about getting the vehicle fixed as much as it was about never admitting that lack of sleep could ever have an effect on my personal wellbeing. This wasn't' the first time sleep deprivation resulted in me wrecking a vehicle. It would not be the last.

A few weeks passed without further incident. Each morning I'd add a day to the mental board in the back of my brain, "Now 31 days injury and accident free" it read. Upon brushing my teeth however, I noticed resistance when I attempted to twist the toothbrush to clean my wisdom teeth. It was a subtle problem, but noticeable enough to cause concern. I blew it off and went on into work.

My nights had been centered around internal discussions on current projects, dealing with shipping and receiving personnel and the occasional misguided stumble down the path of, "Who are we, why are we here and where does the Universe end?"

By lunch, I was in an Applebee's bathroom, staring into the mirror with a finger in my mouth attempting to measure the gap my teeth made. I was sure that my jaw was unable to fully open now. Fitting two fingers stacked into my open mouth was impossible. No wonder I was having trouble eating my hamburger. There was definitely something wrong.

By the next morning, I couldn't open my mouth wide enough to fit a straw. Instead of driving to work, I drove to my dentist.

"I need to shee Doctor Colshun as shoon as poshible," I mumbled through clenched teeth.

"We don't have any open appointments today, I'm sorry." She looked through her calendar. "Next Thursday at 9:00am is our next open appointment."

"No, you don't undershtand. I can't open my mouth at all. I musht have an abssessed toof."

"Wait right here one second." She got up, hid a smile and left, presumably to find Dr Colson.

An hour later, x-rays completed, I sat in the chair waiting for Dr Colson to return with the verdict. "Well, Travis... how's work going?"

"Itsh going. Why?"

"You do *not* have an abscessed wisdom tooth like we assumed. In fact, your mouth is perfectly fine. What it looks like is TMJ." He paused, waiting for a response. None came. "You have lockjaw. Are you under a lot of stress? How's work? How's the wife and kids?" he asked.

"I haven't had lockjaw shinsh junior high." I took a deep breath unable to decide which was better.

"The last time you experienced lock jaw I remember your mother being very upset at the stress you were putting yourself under with school." Dr Colson flipped through my dental charts. "I think it's time you take a good look at your current lifestyle and work habits. I can only prescribe an anti-depressant at this time to help alleviate the lockjaw. Knowing that you've refused Novocain for fillings in the past, I'm assuming there's no way you'd fill that prescription anyway."

"You'd be correct." I answered.

Two week's vacation and a personal promise to make some changes before this got out of hand again, helped correct the immediate problem.

CHAPTER 26

THE MAN IN THE MIRROR

Katherine opened the door and allowed me to pass back into her office. "How have you been?" she asked, trying to get me to smile. "Fine. It's not like I can go anywhere." I walked over and took my seat back on the couch. After I had left, Katherine had put the office back to its normal setting. I stared at the coffee table. "Let's talk more about the religious implications into your fear," she suggested. "Let's not and say we did," I counter offered. She forced a laugh then continued, "What about time travel? Why would you compare time travel to religious beliefs? That seemed very odd."

I looked at her, trying to decide the best way to continue. "Do you believe in time travel?" I asked. "I've never really thought about it," she answered honestly. "Like I said before, the most likely scenario explaining why time travel does not exist in the future would be that the world ends soon. Maybe that's why the technology for time travel will never be invented." I looked back down at the back of my thumb. "Do you think the world is going to end?" she asked. "What does your God say about that?" I retorted. "That would be a pointless discussion now wouldn't it?" she asked with a stern voice. "Not near as pointless as your belief in an imaginary all powerful deity perched above the clouds." She did not see the humor...

The lockjaw finally went away and I was once again able to open my mouth wide enough to fit in an oversized hamburger and bun. Regardless of my continued efforts, I still found myself dealing with increased stress from time to time. The insomnia would always be a factor and my co-pilot would come and go as he pleased. Mostly to help manipulate my major decision making processes. I was as good as could be expected.

A couple days after my twenty-fifth birthday, I stepped out

of the shower and dropped my towel. I looked in the mirror at the end of the hallway on the back wall of the spare bedroom and didn't recognize the guy bending over. He looked like me, only super sized. It was the first time I really looked at myself since High School. I'd always been short, relatively stocky, but very healthy in appearance and physical conditioning. The guy staring back at me through the mirror was none of the above.

I bought a scale on the way home from work.

I placed the scale on the bathroom floor and stared at it helplessly.

"Wait, don't get on it until you take a shower. You'll sweat off a pound or two and maybe wash off a few ounces of dirt."

I jumped in the shower and dried myself thoroughly. I stood in front of the scale and stared at it helplessly.

"Wait, take a piss and shit if you can. You never know."

I did just that then stood in front of the scale and stared at it helplessly.

"Just do it. Get on the damn thing already. You're not getting any thinner."

I took a deep breath and stepped onto the scale. The number 258.8 stared back at me.

"What the fuck? Is this kilograms or some shit?" I asked.

"Nope. You're just fat. I've been trying to warn you, but you don't listen to me anymore."

"What do I do?" I asked desperately.

"We go see your doctor. You need to get this taken care of sooner rather than later. I've got plans for you and if you die young, we're both fucked."

Two days later, I sat on an exam table with my shirt off as my doctor directed my breathing. "Two more. And, inhale... Ok, exhale. And inhale... ok, exhale." He stepped over to the little built in counter covered in more pharmaceutical advertisements than a NASCAR Taurus.

"How bad is it?" I asked.

"You've gained seventy pounds in three years. Your body is showing signs of increased wear. Your blood work came back showing concerns of high blood pressure and dangerous cholesterol levels. I see in your chart that there is a permanent issue of... let me see... looks like sleep apnea? Is that correct?" he asked.

"Sleep apnea? No." I was confused.

"Insomnia?"

"Yeah, I'm a chronic insomniac. Have been since I was a kid. I've never had sleep apnea though. No clue what that was about."

He looked back in my chart. "Insomnia... that makes more sense. Although, I do see sleep apnea in your future... Ok, to answer your question, how bad is it?... it's bad. It's real bad considering you're only twenty-five. You have the body of a forty year old. You need to take better care of yourself." He crossed his arms and shook his head slowly. "This is a failure to recognize common sense."

"What do I need to do then?" The word 'failure' was already weighing on my shoulders.

"You need to go on a *diet*. That's the first thing." The lilt in his tone was ripe with condescension. "You need to cut out the Cola or at least switch to Diet. You need to start exercising on a regular basis. A diet and a regular exercise plan will get you back in normal limits within a couple of years. *If* you stick with it."

The word "failure" burned itself into my psyche. The next day I called my insurance company and set up a physical for a new life insurance policy. The next six months started a new lifestyle. Within a year, I was approved for new insurance and fifty pounds lighter. I even started meeting with a dietician on Tuesdays to help maintain my weight and eating habits. I wasn't going to let questions about existence run my life and now my body as well.

Much like everything else in my life, I became obsessed with exercise. Over the next year I took up running, cardio training, plyometrics and lifting weights. I began running 5K's. Then 10K's. I completed several triathlons and a half marathon before I over worked my body and tore both my ACL and meniscus.

A cadaver tendon, surgery, twelve weeks of physical therapy and the occasional pepperoni pizza with light sauce and extra cheese finally pulled me out of the fanatically fit and dropped me back in the realm of the intelligent exercise and diet.

CHAPTER 27

PARENTHOOD

"Belittling someone's belief is very rude, young man." Katherine sat rigid, staring directly at me. I'd found her button. Deep inside I knew it was wrong to press, but I just couldn't help it. *"I'm not belittling your belief. I'm simply pointing out that I was mistaken."* I tried my best to contain the smile, hoping she'd take the bait. *"Mistaken about what?"* she asked. *"I thought you were my equal. Apparently I was mistaken. There is definitely no point in discussing this further because you're obviously incapable of…"* She stood up before I could complete my sentence and approached her

desk. *"...incapable of seeing what I have to say as anything other than nonsense and I, the like, in turn."* She pressed down on the intercom button, *"Christie, can you get Travis's mother on the phone? We are going to cut today's session a bit short today."* Over the intercom, the voice crackled a reply, *"I'll send her back. She's sitting out in the lobby waiting"...*

"I think it's about time you start spitting out some kids."

"You too?" Apparently I was going to be pressured from all sides.

"It's time."

"I hate this absolution. I hate these ultimatums. I'm arguing with my co-pilot now because the stress of life just isn't enough?" I asked.

"How old are you?"

"I'm twenty-five. What does that have to do with anything?" This line of questioning was getting redundant.

"For longer than you can possibly comprehend, I've worked through these life situations with you, and in every single instance, the outcome has felt, how?"

I thought about it for a moment. "Right? Somehow."

"Exactly, they all feel right..."

"But they don't!" I railroaded the conversation. "They feel predetermined. Like I've been here before. That's not '*right*', that's deja vu."

"Never you mind. You've done gone and missed your window for salvation, it's time you buck up and take the merry-go-round for one more spin."

I always made life-changing decisions through sleep-deprived blinders. Becoming a parent would be no different. Before long I was staring down at a beautiful baby boy and every moment of hesitation seemed to float away on a coo and a smile.

The moment I became a parent also marked an internal shift of power. Every decision I would make from that moment forth would first and foremost be made with his wellbeing in mind. Any illusion I had previously locked away that I was in charge, vanished with his first tear.

Four years later, I'd make the same concession and the same ultimate realization of renewed purpose. Both boys were planned to the day as was with everything in my life.

Now, with two small boys under my wing, I started to see glimpses of myself. Every parent hopes and expects to see such inherent traits. It's only natural. The things I started to recognize, however, were the things that changed my life forever. We noticed heightened intelligence in my oldest right away. He spoke months before the other children we were acquainted with. He established addition and subtraction per cause and effect while his peers were still trying to reign in counting to ten. The night he couldn't go to sleep because he was up worrying, as a five year old, about the realization of his own mortality was the moment I knew he was going to follow down my path. Soon after, because of state mandated testing, he was evaluated for the gifted program in our school system. His cognitive score landed him a lone spot among the rest of the school system. He scored high enough on the test to be added to both Reading and Math programs, but his cognitive score and IQ were high enough that it justified a separate program.

"Should I allow him to do this?" I asked.

"Yes. Otherwise he'll be bored."

"But am I leading him down the path I traveled? I don't want him to miss out on his childhood." I weighed the decision.

"You won't let that happen. You're smart and can see the signs."

"It's a slippery slope," I said.

"Keep one hand on the rail."

A few years later, my youngest started to show similar but different characteristics. His intelligence level was comparable but his attitude and wit were much darker. Instead of finding his joy in accomplishments and success, he was most proud of the discontent and disarray he left in his wake. He has always been entertained by the frustrations of others. He was evil. Not kill-the-neighborhood-cats-evil, but what-can-I-do-to-push-this-situation-over-the-edge-of-a-cliff-evil. He's a ladies man on top of it all. At three years old he announced that his favorite restaurant was Hooter's, but he only wanted hugs from the blonde waitresses. Apparently he's picky too.

His mind has also taken him to the darker questions of reality. I was called into his bedroom during the middle of the night to answer the question, "how long until I die?" Reassuring him that it would be a very long time, many, many years from now only prompted a final retort. "It's okay Dad, you can just say that you don't know. No one knows." How do you respond to that?

When he was four years old we decided to have him tested for admission to kindergarten and follow in his brother's footsteps. He was already reading, could add and subtract as well as showed signs of the same intellect that his sibling had demonstrated at the same developmental age. I dropped him off with the other five year olds so he could go through the hour-long test. Upon picking him back up, I was told I needed to have a conversation with the coordinator in charge. I waited around until everyone else had left, then approached the coordinator.

Good news? Is he smart? I sat down with the handful of teachers administering the test and the coordinator in charge. "How did he do?" I asked.

"Have you ever had him tested before?" the coordinator replied. She was well into her sixties and appeared jovial and good humored. I assumed she was a retired teacher because she seemed right at home in her tiny desk chair.

"No, we just assumed since his brother did so well, we'd give him the same opportunity." I smothered a smile.

"I really don't know how to put this," she stalled... "He didn't pass."

"No, that's fine. No problem at all. He's very young, we'll bring him back next year." I tried to control my astonishment.

The first teacher, a younger woman, maybe pushing thirty, with bright eyes and an earnest smile, leaned across the table. "Honestly, we couldn't even register him. Based on the type of evaluation we use, we didn't know how to score him at all. We can tell he's smart, but it was as if he found joy in frustrating us."

"I'm really confused here. What the heck happened?" I asked.

"He refused to answer our questions honestly, to begin with." The coordinator shuffled through her papers then continued, "Here, let me show you. When asked what animal barks, he replied 'a frog'. When asked how many days were in a week, he answered 'all of them'. It goes on like that for the entire test."

The second teacher, a much older woman with a stern brow picked up. "Some of his answers... we don't even know *where* he came up with them. For example, we asked to name something shiny that a woman puts on her finger, his answer... 'a band-aid'. Which is a creative answer, but not the one we were looking for. After prompting him for a better answer, he said 'nail polish'." She paused for effect or maybe waiting for a response. "It was if he wanted to give us every answer **but** the right one."

"We asked him what holds cereal and he answered 'milk'. We were looking for bowl. We asked him if he could tell us his address and he said 'No, because you're a stranger'. We could not convince him otherwise." The first teacher seemed frustrated simply recounting the events.

"I really don't know what to say. Do you want us to ask him the questions? I'm sure he'll answer for me." I looked over at my son, drawing quietly at a corner table.

The coordinator noticed my attention shift. "His dexterity was excellent and he passed everything else, but when it came to the cognitive questions, he scored a zero. When we asked if he could count to ten, he refused."

"He said he didn't know how?" I turned back to meet the coordinator's eyes.

"Yes. Well, he actually said, 'Yes'. But he wouldn't count. We asked him if he could, he said yes. We asked him if he would and he said he didn't feel like it right then." The coordinator sat back in her chair and crossed her arms. Her casual dress and demeanor contradicted her new attitude. This seasoned professional seemed taken aback by the interaction with my son.

"What does this all mean?" I asked.

"It means we feel sorry for the teacher that gets him in the fall. He's a handful, but we're going to go ahead and pass him." The coordinator leaned forward and smiled.

"Thank you?" I grabbed my son and took my leave.

That night, I asked him what happened at the testing. His reply, "Those teachers were stupid. They asked me dumb questions. I figured if they didn't know the answers, I wasn't gonna tell 'em... Dad, they didn't know what animal barked. They even assumed every question had only one right answer. What are they gonna be able to teach me? I'm not going to school."

CHAPTER 28

FADE TO BLACK

The look on Katherine's face shifted to dismay, then quickly returned to business, "Thank you, send her in." She moved over to the door, and opened it half way, peered out down the hall, then returned to her desk to shuffle papers and reorganize briefly. As my mom reached the doorway, Katherine clasped her hands in front of her and smiled wide. "Knock, knock?" my mother called shyly before she crossed the threshold into my realm. "Come in, come in." Katherine stood and met my mom as she made her way across the carpet toward the empty chair next to the couch. "So nice to see you, again... um...." her words slowed and trailed off before my mother could interject.

"Judy. How is Travis doing? Is everything ok?" Katherine sighed and went back to her perch behind the desk. The picturesque element of authority behind the oversized piece of solid oak screamed superiority complex. Hopefully I'd remember that so I could call her on it sometime down the road. "I think we may be at a crossroads here. I've done everything within my power to help your son work through his crippling fears. I've reached a point where, without his full cooperation, proceeding further is pointless. I'm looking for help on your part to see if we can get him back on track." She offered a palm out in my direction to emphasize what she was establishing as 'the problem'...

As thirty loomed in the not so distant future, so did my failed dreams. I was still moderately successful as a designer. I was raising two amazing sons. I (along with the help of a few friends) had developed and maintained a thriving Internet venture that was starting to gain national attention. I was also managing a small record label with four signed bands. On paper, everything was hunky dory. In my head, however, the world was crashing all around.

I was leading a double life. The outward appearance was that of a successful young man following the American dream to fruitful pastures. The inward reality was a young man on the precipice of disaster and self-destruction. My stress levels were at an all time high. I had so many irons in the fire that I couldn't touch any of them without burning my hand on the next. I was stretched so thin that a hiccup could shred me to bits. With stress comes self-reflection. With self-reflection comes questions. With questions comes fear. With fear comes insomnia. With insomnia comes the spiral to rock bottom.

My climb upward lost momentum until it stalled and I started getting knocked down branch by branch. I soon found myself standing on the last limb, hoping not to fall out of the tree all together. I'd go days with nothing more than a nap in the car at lunch. Sometimes those naps were impromptu and ended with me waking up to a spilled drink and a ruined outfit. Other days, I'd fall asleep at my desk or on the phone. I became a master at fielding questions like, "Where did you go?" and "Did I lose you there?"

I had decided earlier that year to try and pursue my dream of becoming a writer. With the big three-oh looming on the horizon, I felt it was my last chance to say I accomplished something great. I was met with minor success right away and picked up a literary agent with little effort. My nights were spent in my office, staring at a computer screen, trying to spit paisleys all over a rough zombie manifesto. The piece would be my crowning achievement. My Citizen

Kane.

The reality was, I spent more nights drooling into my keyboard and waking up to thirty-six pages of j's than I did producing anything productive. I started losing time during the day. I hadn't blacked out and experienced micronaps since college. Now, nearly a decade later, I once again frequently found myself in the middle of conversations which I soon realized I had no idea how had begun or deep in a discussion based on a conversation I didn't remember even having. I'd drive to work, look up and not remember getting out of bed. All of a sudden my brain would focus on pouring a cup of coffee and I'd be petrified, not knowing where I was or how I'd gotten there.

My mind was finding relief whether I gave it rest or not. Things really started to take a turn for the worse when I woke up at a roadside rest one morning having a panic attack.

"Wake up!"

"What?" I asked.

"I said, wake up!"

"I am." I yawned and opened my eyes.

In front of me, inches from the front bumper, was a massive oak tree. I slammed down on the brake pedal and swerved the wheel from side to side as hard as I could but it wouldn't budge. Pumping the break, I closed my eyes, gritted my teeth, braced for impact and prepared to die. My entire body contracted until the every muscle ached with strain. I screamed and waited for the end.

Nothing happened. The end never came.

I slowly relaxed and opened my left eye a crack before unsquinting the right. In front of me, inches from the front bumper, was a massive oak tree. The tree didn't move. I looked around and allowed my brain to take in the scene. I was stopped off of the interstate alongside the highway, parked in front of a tree on the outskirts of a roadside rest. I slowly looked over to my left. My window was down. In the car next to me sat a young girl, maybe six years old, wide eyed, staring back at me in sheer astonishment. She turned her attention back to the dash in front of her and cranked up her window without looking back in my direction.

I had no idea how I'd gotten to the rest area, let alone the parking spot. I backtracked through my memories to the last thing I recognized. I'd left the house that morning. I remembered getting in the car with my coffee. The last three hours were a complete blank.

These black spots in my memory became more and more frequent. Many times, they came while I was behind the wheel of a car or doing something monotonous. I began to fear for my safety and what the possible outcome would do to my kids.

"Don't worry, I'll keep you out of trouble."

"That's what I'm afraid of."

CHAPTER 29

WHAT DREAMS MAY COME

"What exactly is he doing? Or not doing, rather?"
My mother asked while staring holes through my
flesh with laser eyes. I gave her my best, most
innocent look of "What? I'm the victim here."
Katherine turned her gaze upon me as well, "He's
not doing anything that isn't expected. He feels
threatened and is establishing boundaries. What
I'm trying to explain is I think he may have decided
that I'm unable to help him further. If he's not
willing to allow me in, we are just spinning our
wheels here and wasting mom and dad's money. I
cannot, in good conscience, continue treating your

son without bringing this to your attention. I hope this hasn't discouraged you, I'm really only looking for some parental assistance on your part to make sure he keeps his sleep journal in tact and that when he does attend our sessions each week, he comes well rested and ready to make a genuine effort to find the answers you both seek…"

The thing I missed most about normal sleep was the ability to dream.

Being a chronic insomniac, when I did finally fall asleep, I become dead in the brain. There was (is) nothing going on upstairs besides a reset, restart and deep recharge.

Normal people plug their phone in every night whether or not the battery is even low. Recharging the battery goes quick and leaves the phone able to multi-task. It can take calls, receive emails and continue working on behalf of you as your body lies sleeping. Now, let that same cell phone die completely, then throw it on the charger and go to bed. That's my brain, taking most of the down time to restart. Then, when I get back up, there's no multi-tasking taking place. I even have to slowly start up every single app, just to get my life back in order.

When I would hear people discussing their dreams and reliving their nightmares around the water cooler, I'd get horribly jealous. I'd lay down every night, thoughts and questions racing through my brain, a smile in my mind's eye, willing myself to dream.

I would wake up a few hours later, confused, inevitably taking ten or more minutes to acclimate to my surroundings. Remember who and where I am as well as calm down from the panic that comes with sleep for an insomniac. "How long did I sleep? What did I miss? What day is it?" Sometimes it was scary as hell.

Dreams were never part of the ritual.

Each night, the routine repeated. The morning was met with confusion and I'd spend the rest of the day trying to lock positive thoughts into my subconscious in an effort to find a dream or two the next night.

I took steps to force things. I'd fall asleep with various movies on in the background. Sometimes comedy, other times horror. Anything to evoke a mental response. Music? I tried without success as well. I even attempted falling asleep with ambient pornography, but quickly thought better of it for fear of one of my sons coming in looking for assistance in the wee hours.

After digging deeper, I discovered that certain foods could trigger nightmares; fat free milk, ice cream, chocolate... no results. I tried artificial sweeteners such as Aspartame, NutraSweet and Splenda. The dreams would not come, no matter what.

"Why do you want to dream so bad?"

"It sounds fantastic, that's why..." I said.

"I don't get it. What's the appeal?"

"An alternate reality where I can experience things I can't here? How does that *not* sound fascinating?" I asked myself with astonished glee.

*"What do you call **life** then?"*

"I call it *life*. What I'm looking for is something different. I'm bored with *life*. I feel like I've done this all before. I need something new."

"Dreams won't give you something new."

"I don't *know* that until I *can* know that." The thought trailed off into yet another night of black nothing.

Or did it? Something had changed. After getting out of bed the next morning, I realized I did, without a doubt, dream! I knew I did, I could feel it... but I couldn't remember a single sliver of it. I didn't even know who was in it or if it was a nightmare or a wet dream. I just knew that I did, without a damn doubt, dream! I spent the entire day trying to squeeze a coherent thought to the surface of my mind like I was popping a mental pimple. The need to remember drove me to a state of frenzied madness.

"It's right there, I can almost see it..."

"Frustrating isn't it?"

"More than you know," I replied.

"No. I know. I know. All. Too. Well."

"Why can't you help here?" I pulled the friend card.

"I'm doing my best to help you remember. I always have."

Each night, the routine repeated. The morning was still met with confusion but instead of spending the day trying to find a way to dream the following night, I was trying to lock onto an image from the night before. I would get momentary flashes of... something... but I was unable to grasp a coherent thought.

I was dreaming. Now I needed to remember.

CHAPTER 30

MISERY LOVES COMPANY

Katherine smiled warmly, allowing the sincerity to reach all the way up to her eyes. She waited patiently for a response from my mother who was still focused intently on me. I watched as my mom's rage filled eyes narrowed and the thin line between her lips started to curl on the far outer edge. She turned her piercing stare from me back to the waiting woman. Upon seeing the same expression I'd just witnessed, Katherine's smile faltered. "You hope he comes well rested? Do you even know why I'm bringing him here?" Katherine started to interrupt, but my mother simply spoke over her stammering interjection. "This sounds more like an attack on my parenting than a cry for help. Or is this simply you throwing your hands in the air in defeat, using my son as the scapegoat?" She stood and turned back to me. "Are you ready?" she asked. I stood and started for the door. "I'd like you to think about what I said. When I bring him back next week, I'll come in with him. You can let me know at that time whether or not you feel you've reached your professional limit. I understand he may be difficult to deal with at times. This is why he is here, after all." My mother followed behind me, except she opted to shut the door to Katherine's office behind her, effectively cutting off the rebuttal that had already begun...

Because of what I do for a living, I'm always surrounded by creative individuals. They come and go both in my professional life and in my personal life. Regardless of what they're paid to do or how they title themselves, not all creative individuals are artists. Because of how I live my life, I both attract and crave the attention of artists. All artists are creative individuals, not all creative individuals are artists.

The true artist lives a life completely for, and encompassed by, their own creativity. Every moment of every day is leading toward the artist's next moment of genius. The artist is usually single, obsessive, eccentric and one bad night away from rock bottom. They are almost always addicted to multiple vices and use said crutches as tools to leap frog from project to creation to epiphany to solution to release.

Suicide and self-destruction are also likely side effects to a life spiraling toward the tornadic center of genius. With art comes depression. My theory has always been that when the soul is able to open up and splinter itself, throwing the pieces into the world for everyone to be affected, the creator is left broken. Post partum comes with more than just pregnancy.

Surrounding yourself with these kinds of people can be wonderful and horrible all at the same time. Misery loves company, creativity is infectious, and I was constantly inspired.

Inspiration was not always a good thing, however. I was attending as many funerals and interventions as I did concerts, gallery openings and performances. The creativity was rubbing off on me, but the gloom and depression were as well.

The deeper the depression, the more active my apeirophobia became. By my thirty-first birthday I was nearly nighttime agoraphobic because of the constant reminder the star filled sky provided. I stopped sleeping in a bed altogether. The only rest I received was hunched over a desk or flat on my back sprawled across the office floor. I became anti-social and loathed any and all human contact outside my own immediate family. I started to shut doors and burn bridges, leaving a wake of hurt and confused friends and relatives looking on in stunned silence.

"You need to snap out of this."

"I'm fine," I rationalized.

"No, you're not. This is not going well."

"I'm fine," I tried to convince myself.

"This is not fine. You're on a one-way train to a dixie cup full of anti-psychotics and a repeating routine of staring out the window at an empty bird feeder trying to figure out which one flew over the cuckoo's nest while you wait patiently for your lobotomy."

"I'm fine." This became my catch phrase. My credo. My downfall.

"Can I make a suggestion?"

"Can I stop you?" I asked.

"You need to find an outlet. You need a hobby."

"Suggestions?" I asked, curious where this was going.

"I think it's time to start writing again."

CHAPTER 31

RELEASE

The following week, I found myself sitting in Katherine's office next to my mother, across from a much smaller woman no longer smiling behind a big oversized desk. Katherine had traded in the show of superiority for a servant's persona. I wondered if her contrived tactics were performed on purpose or simple sad cliché. "I have discussed with another colleague your son's case... I say 'case' because I feel that the problems he is facing are not as easily fixed as finding a suppressed memory or facing a fear. This is where everyone who has seen him before has come to an end I am

assuming?" My mother nodded, "More or less."
Katherine stood and walked around to her desk.
"That being said, I'd like to present you with
another possibility. The colleague I referred Travis
to is currently working on a research study for
gifted children at the University. The person in
charge is a brilliant therapist who specializes in
cases similar to your son's. We spoke over the
phone and think that Travis would make an
excellent addition to the study. The theory is to
reprogram the brain to ignore the fear and
questions that bother him through hypnosis"...

I had stopped writing the novel I'd begun a few years
earlier when the literary agent who had approached me
was hired by another firm and in turn left me with false
promises and well wishes. I had been interested in
creative writing since I was very young. Spending hours in
a darkened room, living out the fantasy of being trapped in
Croatoan, I eventually decided it would be cool to start
recording the stories and adventures in a private journal.
Reading them back to myself turned the words in my
tattered red spiral notebook into elaborate films played out
on the tapestry of my mind's eye... At that early age, I
preferred to read a story the way I wanted it to unfold
instead of someone else's fantasy. This eventually drove

me to write.

In college, I'd made fiction writing my minor. I had a few pieces published, but necessity dictated I put my focus on my major. Come graduation, instead of pursuing frivolous dreams into the world as an author, I would settle down as a designer. The internal battle that had kept me on course, waged years before when I had eventually conceded defeat, forced me once again to accept my role as a designer and put other dreams to rest.

"It's not time."

"Why not?" I asked. "I'm still young. Now's the perfect time to take risks."

"It's not the 'right' time."

"It's never going to be the *right* time. I'm looking for *my* time."

"Right now, you need to do what's best for your stability. You'll come back to this. It's in your future, it's just not in your present."

It never felt... right. Becoming a designer... did. It was the correct decision at the time. Now *that* time was in the past and I was standing firmly in *my* future.

"You need to find an outlet. You need a hobby."

"Suggestions?" I asked, curious where this was going.

"I think it's time to start writing again."

Write I did. At first, I picked up the discarded novel I'd left years before. After reading through it and attempting to move forward from where it had previously been abandoned, my heart wasn't in it. It didn't feel right, so I placed it back on the shelf and decided to begin free writing for myself. On the way home from work I stopped and bought an all too familiar spiral notebook.

Putting pen to paper was like spring-cleaning for my psyche. What I wrote was pointless drivel that led nowhere but the purpose wasn't to create something for someone to read. I was priming the pump and finding a release. It worked.

At first...

Eventually the novelty of spilling my inner trials onto paper with no intent for anyone to ever see them became a chore and not a sanctuary. In a fit of rage, I realized I hated the red spiral notebook I was desperately attempting to fill. I walked out into my garage, late one night, kicked a trashcan out of the way and threw a bicycle into the drywall. I cleared a spot on the cement floor among oil stains and curled spider carcasses. I dropped the red notebook in the middle and went for gasoline. The can, empty, arced perfectly into the overturned bicycle. After looking without success among the ruin of the garage for something flammable, I returned to the kitchen and settled for a fifth from the liquor cabinet.

I sat the glass bottle down on the garage floor harder than I should have and knelt next to the notebook. The sound of the concrete kissing the glass sent a shiver up my spine but I continued forward undeterred. My knees screamed in protest as each tiny bit of dirt and gravel buckled under my weight. I picked up the spiral notebook and rolled it in my hand, bending the edges and curling the cover effectively. I threw the wadded mess back to the floor and grabbed the grain alcohol at my side. I turned the white plastic lid and cracked the pressed perforated seal. The smell hit my nose even before the glass touched my lip. One swig from the bottle was more than enough. I breathed deep, cleared my throat and poured a healthy dose of Everclear onto the notebook. Where the splatter marked the concrete on either side, it dried and disappeared without a whimper. Matchbook from my pocket in one hand, the bottle in the other I rocked back onto the balls of my feet and sat the bottle behind me, more gingerly this time. My right hand pulled a match free. My left hand sandwiched it between the cardboard and the striking strip. A second deep breath and I pulled the sword from the stone.

I dropped the matchbook onto the notebook and followed it with the searing match. As soon as the flame touched the doused notebook, the pyre came to life. Immediately I took another step back on bending knees.

Watching the red notebook burn bright and true, my head started to swim. The effigy twisted under the grip of the flames, curling and writhing on the floor as it left this world, taking my words with it until the only thing left was a pile of ash and a screaming smoke detector overhead.

I'd been here before. I'd done this before.

Memories came swimming back to the surface of burning the same tattered red spiral notebook years before. Lifetimes before. I ran to the connecting door and pressed the lit button marked "Genie". No magic words were uttered yet the overhead door came to life, creaking and moaning as it rolled up and pulled back above the rising smoke. I ran for fresh air, my vision twisting, my head spinning. I leaned over the porch railing and let go of everything I'd been keeping pent up inside. Vomit gave way to a scream and tears.

"Are you ok? You seem a little upset."

"FUCK YOU!" I screamed.

"Is this a bad time?"

"This is a very bad time." I calmed down a bit.

"You should feel better."

I thought about that for a minute. "I do actually."

"I think it's time to start writing again."

"What the fuck have I been doing?" I asked.

"You've been purging the system. Priming the pump.

Scraping off the head. That wasn't writing... that was cleaning."

"This all seems too familiar," I mused, "I've been here before."

"Yes, we have. Many, many times before."

CHAPTER 32

I THINK THEREFORE I AM

Katherine took a drink of water and continued, "I can already tell that you're skeptical, but please hear me out. The nature of Travis's fear lies in the unknown. It's difficult, to say the least, for someone to face and accept a fear when the fear itself is of..." She paused for dramatic effect, "...the unknown. I think this is the best possible option for Travis. It's your decision, as always. Also, I should point out, that if you do accept the offer and sign a waiver allowing Travis to be used as part of a case study for other children facing the same or similar problems, the therapy sessions will be free of charge until the study has completed. Please mull it over and let me know as soon as possible so I can call Dr Schicksal." My mother listened to Katherine's spiel with a perfect poker face. When she was finally finished talking, my mother simply stood, patted me on the shoulder and crossed to the door. She paused and spoke over her shoulder. "We'll let you know in the next day or so how we plan to proceed." My mother straightened and headed down the hall, expecting me to follow. Follow I did, pausing momentarily in the doorway to speak over my shoulder as well, "I told you that you'd eventually give up on me. Everyone gives up on me." I walked out and pulled the door shut behind me effectively cutting off the rebuttal that had already begun…

After the funeral in my garage, I spent three days in a hole. No contact with another human whatsoever. I left a note on the table (actually it was a plea and an apology) and jumped in my car, driving 1,000 miles south to spend a few days alone in the condo I'd bought a couple years prior. The condo itself was a joke. My co-pilot had begged for a place to go. He had sworn we needed a secret cave to escape to, just the two of us. At the time, it seemed

270

frivolous and unnecessary, but he had convinced me otherwise.

"Just drive."

"Where?" I asked.

"The fortress of solitude beckons."

"I hate Superman. I *really* hate Superman." I really disliked super hero stories, super hero comics, super hero movies, super hero everything.

"I know, that's why I find it entertaining to push you in that direction."

"Why?" I asked. "Why push me? Why now?"

"Now is the time. Now is the right time. We've got work to do."

"What kind of work?" The confusion was setting in.

"Just drive."

I arrived at the condo, checked in, unloaded my car, sat down on the couch and fell asleep.

I slept for hours. Sweet sleep. Sweet relief.

"Wake up."

"I am awake," I said.

"No you're not. Wake up."

"Fuck. I said I was awake," I bit back.

"Oh yeah? Where are you?"

I looked around through one half open eye. The room looked wrong. I sat upright, startled. Both eyes open. "Where am I?" My breathing turned ragged and intense.

"Calm down, everything is ok. You need to breathe."

"Where the fuck *am* I?" I asked again.

*"We're where it all began. Where it all **begins**."*

I looked around again; I was sitting on the couch in a living room that didn't look like a living room at all. It looked like a waiting room. I stood cautiously and walked to the window. I counted in my head the prime sequence that grounded me to the moment. "Two, three, five, seven, eleven, thirteen, seventeen..."

"Take a look. Do it quickly though, we need to get out of here before someone sees us."

"...fifty-three, fifty-nine, sixty-one, sixty-seven..." I peeked through the vertical blinds and saw the front of my BMW parked dangerously close to a yellow fire hydrant on the curb just thirty feet away. The yard was unkempt and filled with more thistle than grass. I stepped back from the window and took another deep breath. The light from the street lamp shining through the parted blinds was momentarily enraged, flooding the room in a bright explosion of white. My pupils narrowed, leaving the room black once again. Slowly the street lamp beyond began to return to its full luminosity as the hint of a rumble erupted overhead. The thunder built to a crescendo, rolling over the house with such force that my window rattled in its frame. The street lamp, irritated by the flash of light, slowly acclimated back to the dark of night, returning the spilled light to the back wall of the room before the next flash of lightning was able to recycle the process all over again. "…one hundred and nine, one hundred thirteen, one hundred twenty-seven, one hundred thirty-one…"

"Do you remember this place?"

"…one hundred forty-nine, one hundred fifty-one, one hundred fifty-seven…"

"You will. Take a moment to get your bearing and slowly walk out the front door and back to the car like you own the place. Trust me."

"…one hundred seventy-three, one hundred seventy-nine…" I did as I was told.

"I thought you were ready. Maybe you're not."

"I think therefore I am. I think therefore I am. I think therefore I am." I repeated the phrase in my head. It was given to me years before, but only now coming back to me. From whence it came, I did not yet know.

*"Yes, I think therefore I am. Exactly… You have no idea **what** you are, do you?"*

"I guess not," I answered.

"Stick with me kid, you'll be just fine."

PART IV

LET THERE BE LIGHT

CHAPTER 33

THE RETURN

I spent the next two weeks drowning out everyone and everything. I didn't want to try to explain to family and friends why I'd driven sixteen hours to Florida, slept for twenty, and then driven sixteen hours back home. I definitely did not want to explain to family and friends that I don't remember sleeping or driving home. I all but blocked out the breaking and entering that had taken place post return.

My co-pilot sat silent. I think he was giving me space. Maybe time to breathe? It didn't matter; the peace and quiet in my head was nice for a change. I will admit that every time I got behind the wheel of my car, it took everything I had to resist the urge to drive back to the house I'd stumbled out of at 2:00am in the pouring rain a few nights before. The house seemed familiar, but unrecognizable. Each time, I pictured it in my head; I drove it back and packed it deeper in the cellar of my subconscious. I was embarrassed and disappointed in myself. I'd lost control. It would not happen again.

"I think we need to talk."

The five most dreaded words to every man with enough intelligence and experience to know how they are most often followed. I ignored them all together.

"I think we need to talk. It's time."

"I don't want to talk. I don't want to talk to you." I shut out the voice and focused on the Rubik's cube I had in my hands. If it wasn't in my hands, it was in my pocket. I'd become so obsessed with the mechanical muse that the sequence to solve its colored conundrum was burned into my brain. My fingers worked it over without the necessity of neural involvement. Bringing it solid over and over again was numbing. Mix it up, solve it, mix it up, solve it. Faster. Do it faster. Do it faster. Just do it.

"It's time."

I ignored.

"I don't want to have to do this the hard way."

I ignored.

"Fine. If you're not going to listen to me, you'll have to listen to him."

I ignored. Again my co-pilot went silent. I think he was giving me space. Maybe time to breathe? It didn't matter; the peace and quiet in my head was nice for a change. For two more weeks, I functioned as a normal adult.

Something pressed down on the end of my king sized bed. My eyes were still closed tight, yet my brain spun up and relayed the sensation optically. Problem was, at this point, I was still too tired to open my eyelids to confirm said phenomenon. The pressure on the mattress was likely my youngest, climbing up onto the bed to let me know he'd wet his own, he couldn't sleep, or that Spongebob was his favorite sea creature. Who knew... but at that very moment, it seemed like a much better idea to pretend to still be lost in dreamland than to open my eyes and face the ascending toddler. After all, if he thought I was fast asleep, maybe he'd go back to his own bed without incident. Wishful thinking.

"Wait a minute, this is way too much weight for my little monster..." I worried. No answer from my co-pilot. The pressure on the end of the bed felt more like a gorilla than a toddler. Still half asleep, I tried to rationalize the situation as my Weimaraner, Dexter, climbing into bed. "Too heavy to be Dexter," I argued with myself for a change.

The mattress collapsed on either side of my stacked legs, rolling me slightly to the side. Making it's way toward my torso, the pressure on the bed felt as if someone was walking up the mattress, straddling me with each footstep. My eyes still shut, half stuck in a dream, I continued to analyze the situation. Until...

What could only be described as a large strong hand gripped my ribs and rolled me onto my back. What was before the state between deep sleep and fighting for consciousness immediately became the state of wide the fuck awake. I tried to sit upright and face my attacker in a startled panic, but was met with a second hand, pressing down on my chest and a third hand covering my eyes in total dark. The same shadowed darkness that had frightened me as a kid.

Since I was a child, I've always had a fear of being tied down. I hate to be pinned or tickled and when faced with such situations, anxiety kicks in and I often experience a panic attack. My breathing became frantic and my heart tried to burst through my chest to report the situation to my still obstructed eyes. My attacker steadied his grip and stance, settled on my chest and removed his hand from my eyes. Completely pinned to my mattress and held in place from my fingertips up to my neck, down my torso, past my waist, all the way to my toes, it felt as if an elephant had fallen asleep across me. Each breath was a struggle and even my heart felt as if it was being crushed under the weight of my own rib cage.

Bravery fought its way to my eyelids and peeled them up and away, revealing a bright overhead light. I tried to focus on the painful brilliance, but could only see a swirl of spots. I tried to thrash and wrestle free, but it was if each and every muscle in my body was on break. The paralysis was painful. My limbs had fallen asleep and the pins and needles were being worked through flesh, through bone, to sample my morrow. I tried to scream but my mouth and vocal chords were also affected by whatever drug had obviously been forced through my veins. The panic attack met a new hurdle and leaped over while the crowd looked on in amazement.

The blinding white light surged brighter, then dimmed, then brighter still before clicking off with a pop as the filament met its breaking point. My pupils at full contraction started to slowly spin outward to a normal operating diameter, allowing the light from my open master bath to spill in over the shoulder of the figure perched on my chest. My eyes slowly adjusted revealing a thick shadow in the shape of a man straddling my chest. His hands on my shoulders pinned me to the bed. Still I could not move.

The incandescent light filtered through his hair like the morning sun winding it's way through bedroom blinds. I tried to focus on the face, but the contrast of shadow and light gave me only a silhouette. As if letting me know he could see me struggle to make out his features, he slowly cocked his head to the left and pressed harder against my chest. My breathing ceased and my heart thumped harder to make up for the loss of sound.

Focusing on the black hole that sat in the middle of his face, it was as if I was gazing into nothing. An empty vacuum stared back. The harder I focused, the more black the face burned. Franticly I looked side to side, as far as my eye could see in my peripheral. Dexter lay beside me still, fast asleep, paying no attention to the black shadow that choked the life from me just inches away.

I returned my attention to the black hole in the center of his face. Maybe because I was looking so intently into the nothing, seeing what I felt should be there, I started to make out tiny pinholes of light. Distant stars in the night sky decorated his face, bringing my heart to a near critical beat. Just then, to my astonishment, he opened his eyes. Wide round orbs of pristine white, veined pink from the corners to a glassed center where the pupil and iris should have been burned holes through me. My heart stopped. All sound faded to a hum as if the air were sucked out of the room.

Tunnel vision started to set in, either because of the pressure on my chest, the panic attack or unadulterated fear. Black engulfed the edges of my sight and narrowed my view until only the two glowing orbs of pristine white remained, like a pair of distant lit doorways. The doors closed, leaving only black. Silence. Nothing.

"I am you." The Shadow Man whispered into my ear. *"Do not be frightened. You bid me to come."* Despite his words,

I *was* frightened; I had never been more frightened in all my life. *"I told you we needed to talk, but you did not listen. Are you listening now? Where is the end to the farthest reaches of space?"* I curled in on myself trying to shut him out as he laughed through dead eyes at my despair.

Then black. Silence. Nothing.

I shot up in bed, my lungs empty and my throat shaking from strain. In the doorway my son stood crying, holding his face. I looked down and realized I'd pissed myself clear through the comforter. It took a moment to realize where I was and that I'd been screaming so loud, I'd woken my son, forced Dexter out of bed and damaged my throat in the process. I calmed down, wiped the sweat from my face and tried to climb to the end of the bed. The light from the bathroom barely illuminated my bedroom. Trying to force my eyes to acclimate to the room, I made my way to my son.

"Calm down, honey. I'm so sorry I woke you up," I said in the most calming voice I could muster in this still rattled state. I bent to comfort my boy and reached up to flip the light on at the same time to facilitate the cleaning and damage control that was about to take place.

Nothing. No pop. No flash of light. The bulb was burnt black.

In the coming week I shared the experience with my mother. I told her it was the scariest dream of my life and that it was so real the thought of it scared me even thinking about it.

"You've had these before, when you were a small boy. Don't you remember? We were taking you to a psychiatrist for your insomnia at the same time so we thought it was all related. They told us it was called Sleep Paralysis. After therapy you never complained about it again."

I was shocked, disgusted, scared and appalled. "I went to a psychiatrist? When?"

She looked at me confused. "When? Don't you remember?"

I did not. "Something like this happened to me when I was a child? What the fuck?" How could I not remember it? In fact, I still didn't.

CHAPTER 34

CONFRONTATION

A few months passed without any new developments. Life carried on. The sun rose and set each day despite the turmoil in my head. Every question I had, old and new, remained unanswered. My brain swam in a sea of static. Pins and needles snaking through my sleeping limbs offered more stimulation than the world around me. The seasons changed and the calendar flipped, yet I could not take notice.

"Why?"

No answer.

Although *I* was lost in my own head, those closest to me were not. They were taking notice and feared a complete mental breakdown. My closest friend, with whom I had spent nearly every waking moment for the last few years, finally mentioned the elephant.

"When are you going to talk to me?" Angie asked.

"About what?" I stuffed the last bite of cheese coney into my mouth.

"You know what I'm talking about. You're not here, your mind is off somewhere and I want to know where." Blunt and to the point... that was Angie.

I picked up my last dog and met my mouth halfway to the plate trying to keep the chili drips to a minimum. As my lips parted to allow entry, she grabbed my wrist and forced the cheese coney back down to my plate. My mouth instinctively followed it until I looked up and noticed the scowl on her face. "Seriously?" I asked.

"Seriously." She released the cheese coney.

Another bite and I put down the remaining half mangled

mess, wiped my hands and sat back in the booth. Out the window a church van pulled up and dumped what appeared to be a youth basketball team at the restaurant's entrance. "I'm just busy." I watched the first boy, the tallest and probably the oldest, hold the door for the rest of the team. In they filed, taking the tables on the other side of the tiny restaurant. I looked down at my plate and thanked them silently for their choice. Screaming kids were not what I needed at that moment.

"I'm just busy? That's your answer?" Angie asked before she dropped her fork back to her plate. She didn't bother keeping her disgust to herself, letting it roll off her tongue with each word.

"I've got a lot going on right now. Ok, fine," I realized she wasn't going to allow the conversation to end like this, "I don't want to talk about it." I dropped my napkin to cover the half eaten monstrosity that used to be my lunch.

"In ten years, I've never seen you leave a plate with food on it." She picked up the napkin and eyed the mess.

"What are you saying? I'm fat?" I tried to lighten the mood.

"In the head." She dropped the napkin. "Let me in,

asshole. I've always been here. I'm your best shot. You know that," her voice softened, "I love you, ya big piece of shit. Just give me a chance to help."

"I know, I know… It's not that easy though." I changed my mind. Why hadn't that group of screaming kids sat over here?

"I offered." She picked up her wallet from the table and grabbed the check. "I'm not real happy with you right now." She stood and walked to the register.

I looked out the window for a few more moments before gathering my keys and meeting her at the register. "I want a peppermint patty too," I said. She didn't look at me, just grabbed one from the jar at eye level and sat it next to me. I picked it up and unwrapped it. "Oh, and can you leave the tip? I don't have any cash."

She sighed heavily and scratched out the receipt, adding a tip before signing her name. "Now I'm REALLY not happy with you." She handed me the receipt and took the keys. "I want reimbursed when we get back to the office."

I followed her out to my car and climbed in the passenger seat. I'd been so tired that morning from lack of sleep, she'd insisted on driving for fear of her own life. I wasn't *that* tired, but I did it rather than listen to her bitch incessantly.

Halfway back to the office, she continued the conversation, "At least tell me if it's the infinity stuff." Only a few people in my life were aware of my personal fears, Angie being one. I'd kept that part of myself locked up and away from ridicule as long as possible, but finally needed to let a few people in for my own sake.

"Sort of." I stared down the barrel and pulled the trigger. "I found out recently that my mom and dad put me in therapy when I was a kid."

"What do you mean *you just found out*?" she asked, never taking her eyes off of the road.

"I think I had buried the memory. I don't know. It's just starting to come back to me." I stared out the window, not daring to catch her gaze.

"Did you ask your parents? How do you know it isn't just your imagination… or a dream?"

"I asked mom. She confirmed."

"hmmm…" She pulled back into our parking lot and turned into my spot outside the back door. "What else did she say?"

"Nothing. I actually asked her about a weird nightmare I had. That was when she told me about the therapy." I unbuckled my belt and reached for the door handle.

"Wait." She grabbed my hand. "You need to talk to your mom. If not for yourself, for me. For all of us. We're worried about you."

I paused and let go of the handle. "Is it that obvious?" I asked.

"Yeah, it is."

I nodded. Angie handed me back my keys.

That night, I drove over to my parents. Angie had offered to go with me, but this was something that I needed to do alone. My father wasn't home, working late, so I sat down at the kitchen table with my mother. "Mom, I need to talk about what you told me a while back."

"What was that?" she asked, sipped her coffee and raised her eyebrows to complete the question.

"About me in therapy when I was a kid. I need to know about it." I waited for her to respond.

"Ok." She sat her coffee cup down and settled into her chair, either out of nervousness or getting ready for a long story, I didn't know. "First you need to know that your father and I had done everything we knew how to do before we went that route. It wasn't like we just sent you off to see a shrink. You weren't sleeping and it was affecting your grades, your attitude. I felt like I was losing my son." A tear formed in the corner of her eye. "I can't believe you don't remember..." her voice cracked. "Was it such a horrible experience that you blocked it completely?" She stood to retrieve a box of tissues having begun to cry.

"I don't know. I just know that all of a sudden it's starting to come back to me. I don't know why but I feel like there's something there that I need to figure out and maybe I'll be better. Or not better, but... I don't know. I just feel like I need to get it out, then decide what to do." I reached for her hand. It was impossible to act intelligent when my mother shed tears.

"Did they touch you? Oh God, were you… *molested?"* she let loose with a wale. "Oh my God, what did we do?" She rolled her head back and up directing the last question at the ceiling.

"Wait, 'they'? How many therapists did I go to? Stop crying, I need to you tell me everything." I was no longer feeling sorry for my mother; her tears were now annoying me. "Mom, this isn't your fault! Mom! Calm down, I just need answers god damn it."

The tone in my voice stopped her self-pity and focused her back at my question. "I'm sorry honey." She wiped her eyes and wrapped her hands around her coffee cup. She breathed deep, fighting back the emotion, then steadied herself. She sat silent for a few minutes, gathering courage before she continued. "Yes, there were several. Most of them lasted only a couple of sessions before they suggested another therapist more qualified to deal with your insomnia. Then again, another referral. And another. Finally you were with a nice young woman named Dr Hill. She spent nearly a year with you before she referred us to a therapist at the University. You met with this new therapist there a while, then back at Dr Hill's office. I can't remember… what was the name? It was German, I think."

"Do you remember?"

"No." I said out loud.

"No?" my mother asked. "I'm not lying. It all happened. I'm sorry you can't…"

"No, I can't remember," I cut her off. "I was talking to myself."

"Do you remember?"

"No I don't remember. That's why I'm here." I said.

"You will. You're close."

"This isn't helping. I need to get the fuck out of here." I said to myself before I stood up. "Thanks, mom." I leaned over and hugged her. "I need to get home."

"I'm glad I could help. I did help didn't I?" she asked.

"Yes, of course you did." I smiled. "I love you."

"I love you too, honey. Kiss my grandkids for me." She stood and followed me to the back door. "Are you ok?"

"I will and yes, I'm fine, I'm just busy." I waved and walked to my car.

"Dr Schicksal."

"What?" I asked.

"That was the name you were looking for... Dr Schicksal."

"Dr Schicksal." I said. "Dr Schicksal." I said out loud.

"You're starting to remember. It's time."

I started the car and pulled out onto the road heading south, away from my house. It was time to put the pieces together.

CHAPTER 35

THE FLOOD

I pulled up the address in the GPS's memory. I'd saved it months ago expecting this day would come. The house was actually much closer to my parents' than I'd previously realized. Within twenty minutes, I was pulled up behind the same fire hydrant I'd nearly hit previously. In the daylight, I could see that the house wasn't really a house at all. It had been converted from a three or four bedroom ranch to a small office. Most recently it had belonged to an herbalist made evident by the neon "COLONIC" hanging out front. Peeling red shutters sat helplessly alongside dirty windows peppered with BB cracks and duct tape. The spouting clung for dear life to the edge of the roof in places, swaying with the breeze in others. Crows lined the peak of the roof, crab walking back and forth, squawking out a chorus of caution. Looking up and down the street in either direction, more dilapidated homes amplified the despair radiating from the property before me. The neighborhood was in ruin and looked more like a set from a made for video apocalypse flick than a forgotten corner of my childhood.

I left my car running, got out and slowly walked up the sidewalk to the front door. The "CLOSED" sign hung crooked behind a piece of paper taped to the inside of the outer door. "NOTICE" it read, followed by a statement from the bank that the home had been foreclosed and seized pending a Sheriff's auction. Based on the date, the notice had been posted months before. I opened the rusted door and stepped closer to the dull red front door.

"So this is it?" I asked. "Should I pop in and get a colonic for old time's sake?"

"This is it. Bring back any memories yet?"

"Nope. Well, *sorta*. I don't know." I cupped my hands over my eyes and peered through the vertical window in the door at the lobby within. There were two chairs, a couch and a receptionist's desk. Nothing fancy but everything did look...

"It does look familiar I guess, but that's probably because I was here, stumbling through the dark, not that long ago." I surmised.

"Yeah, couldn't be because you spent half your childhood here or anything."

"I guess." I said as I walked back down the path. A chill in the air hiked my shoulders toward my ears. I stuffed my hands in my pockets and turned on my heel to look at the house from the sidewalk. I tilted my head and tried to will the memories to the surface. "Familiar..."

"Let it go. You're trying too hard."

I took a step back and leaned against the fender of my car. I pulled my dad's lighter out of my jacket and fished in my back pocket for the tin of cigarillos I'd also snatched from his work bench. He didn't need'em and had supposedly quit already. I smelled the sweet aroma as I placed it between eager lips. I leaned forward, returning the tin to my back pocket as I clicked the butane lighter to life. I pulled the blue flame through the length of tobacco with a steady inhale, snapped the lighter shut and savored the moment.

A car sped by behind me. It shifted gears as it attempted to make a yellow light. I looked up and watched over my shoulder as the screech of tires let me know the light had changed to red sooner rather than later... In that instant, everything seemed to swim back to the surface. The sound of sliding rubber on pavement rang in my ears.

"Déjà vu." I said.

"No such thing."

"I remember this place. I remember Katherine, my therapist." I stood up away from the car and took a step toward the house. "I remember." I took another draw from the cigarillo before sending the smoke on a detour through my nasal cavity.

"It's about fucking time."

Over the next few weeks, more and more memories started to crawl out of the graveyard and return to life. I would bend over and pick up a piece of paper and remember doing the same years before. The smell of popcorn triggered visions. The sound of footsteps on concrete was like a shotgun blast to the locked cellar in my brain. A phrase overheard at the gas station, the smell of perfume, a song on the radio, a motorized wheelchair at the mall... there was no escape. My brain was overflowing with forgotten moments from my childhood.

At first it was amazing, I felt like I was making major headway into the mystery of my past. I was excited because I imagined an a-ha moment when one specific recollection would fix me. I'd be able to sleep at night. I'd stop worrying about my existence, my death... reality. I'd stop questioning the end of the universe and the impossibilities of infinite space. I'd just be me.

I was walking from my office to my car one night after work, running through all of the revelations and vivid memories I'd collected thus far; looking for a pattern, a reason, something.

"You need to slow down."

"Why?" I asked.

"It's too much too fast and now you're starting to expect

things that aren't going to come with it."

"I thought you wanted me to remember? Make up your fucking mind." I said making sure my aggravation was clear.

"It's my mind too and I just don't want you to be too disappointed with what you find. Or don't find."

"I won't be disappointed. I just want answers." I said, calming down.

"Think about this, if you went to the psychiatrists for your insomnia, the problem would have been there before any of your memories are taking place."

"Maybe." I reasoned.

*"No, there is no **maybe.** Your insomnia and fears have nothing to do with what you are trying to remember."*

"Then. What. Is. The POINT?" Rage filled my head.

"You'll know when I want you to know. Now slow down!"

And down I went. Face down, to be exact. Face down onto the sidewalk not five feet from the driver's door of my car.

CHAPTER 36

FINDING SOLACE

"I think social media is the way to go. It's the one big avenue that we've never attempted to tap." Stephanie took another sip from her aluminum coffee mug, then pulled it away from her lips, looked into the lid and tipped it back to her mouth, this time tilting it straight to the ceiling.

"It's empty, hun. Give it a break." Angie tapped Stephanie's hand from across the table. "Are we talking MySpace or what?"

"We've already got the blog, but none of you will help me without being coerced into it with threats and bribes. Wait, did you just say 'MySpace'?" I leaned against the table and looked down at the meeting itinerary to see how many more points we had to go through before I could get back to my desk and continue with the project I was still fighting. Almost a year earlier, I'd started the blog as a place to post my rants and ramblings. We'd decided that I needed an outlet after burning my notebook in the garage.

"That's not fair. I've written plenty," Angie said to the group. "Isn't 'MySpace' still a thing?"

"Jesus Christ you are clueless," Stephanie put her palm to her forehead to exaggerate the faux pas. "MySpace died years ago."

Angie twisted her face into a grimace complete with exposed tongue and crossed eyes.

"Facebook is a fucking joke." Chad stood and walked to the trashcan to throw in his empty energy drink and grab another from the mini fridge in the corner.

"I'm talking about Twitter," Stephanie offered. "There's a complete portion of it devoted entirely to offensive jokes and quips. It's perfect. We tell a few jokes, sell a few shirts. I think it's worth a shot."

"Are you offering?" I asked.

"No. Huh? Me? No. Umm, I was assuming you'd do it," she stammered forth. I'd caught her off guard suggesting just the opposite.

"I don't have the time or the patience. What about Ang?" I turned to her and pointed as if I'd caught her with her hand in the cookie jar.

"Me? I don't even have a face book page thing. Fuck. I'm not funny!" she demanded.

"You don't have to be funny. I think we'd get more action from you being a pervert," Stephanie said with a snort.

"Ok, well, *that* I can do." Angie turned to me. "One condition. You and Travis do it with me."

"Fine," Stephanie said. "We'll run it together that way we're not consumed by it."

"*Fine?* I'm not agreeing to any of this." I crossed my arms and sat upright.

"Just smile and say ok," Chad said as he walked behind me. "They'll never let you back out now. Just agree. I've got shit to do."

That was it; I was introduced to social media. Within three months, we'd splintered the one joint account into two separate accounts: Angie running one, myself in control of the other. Stephanie attempted (and failed) to crack into the Facebook demographic. I hated it at first. Being funny and interesting was a chore. Angie, however, took to it like a fish to water.

I tried to get out of the obligation multiple times, but through her constant begging and complaining it was easier to keep it alive than it was to shut it down and listen to her complain.

Then, I started to make fond acquaintances. My closest friends had always been a strange lot. Adding in the incredibly talented and interesting family I was slowly becoming a part of on the Internet and I felt more included in the group than I had in a very long time. The future was looking positive.

I started to confide in my closest online friends. I felt comfortable telling total strangers things that I'd held deep inside me my entire life. There was something intimate and anonymous about talking to these imaginary friends who I never planned on meeting in person. I even developed deep, and what I hope to be lasting, friendships with some of them. I found that my ability to be social was much easier when proximity was not a factor. These amazing people who lived on the other side of my LCD screen became my surrogate family.

One night my closest friend suggested I try Tumblr. Telling some of my stories in the micro blog format could be fun. I checked it out and decided to give it a shot. I started to post jokes, funny pictures and stories to get a laugh or two.

A few months passed and I found myself lying awake at night, going back to old dark places. My mind raced to unanswered questions. Why am I here? What is the Universe? Where does it end? What is the point? The hallucinations returned. The shadows would find me in the dark of night. I spiraled back to my darkest days within a few weeks.

In the wee hours of the morning, instead of lying in bed drowning in my own head, I decided to start writing. I explained my fears and spilled my guts on my insomnia. I let loose secrets I'd kept to myself for years. At first, it felt good to just get the words out of my head. Soon though, people started to respond, ask questions and tell similar secrets. Knowing someone out there was reading what I was writing was liberating. Knowing someone out there could relate to my issues was inspiring.

"Are you ready to start talking about what you know and what you've found out?"

"Why would I?" I asked.

"This is what we have to do. This is why I'm here."

"What? Go back to therapy? Fuck that." I had no intention of ever going down that path again.

"No. Use the Internet as therapy. You need to tell your story."

"I don't know my story. There are still so many holes."

"What if I were to tell you the story?"

"Huh?"

"It's time I let you in on the secret."

CHAPTER 37

THE REVEAL

"What secret?" I asked.

"The same secret I've told you time and time again. Nothing changes. No matter how much I want it to, each time I find myself here, in this same situation, trying to plan better for the next time through."

"You lost me."

"I lost you lifetimes ago."

"Lifetimes? You're making no sense." Now I was more

than confused.

"When you were seven years old and The Shadow Man visited you the first time in your bedroom, I needed you to fight. I needed you to get through all of this on your own."

"What time are you talking about?" My pulse started to speed up, my breathing became labored.

"Calm down and shut the fuck up. Now's the time to listen not ask more questions. Now is the time. When you started to go to the dark place in your head, The Shadow Man visited you in your bedroom. When the sleep evaded you long enough you could see beyond this life… he took advantage. I can help, but I can't intervene. I told you not to be afraid, but your head was already lost to the dark. I did everything I could to keep you from yourself. No matter what I tried, you kept me locked away. I tried to escape. If only I could have broken through, things may have been different."

I inhaled deep, my heart fluttered and the blood pounded through my ears.

"You need to calm down. You need to count. Prime numbers, remember your numbers… stay with me. I need

you to understand."

The panic attack continued despite my efforts.

"I'll make it quick. You've been a tool for so long, I've lost track. I'm going to show you, make you remember. Then it's up to you to tell your story. You must tell your story. It's the only way. You must go through in order to make it out. I need just one more chance to put things right."

"Breathe… just breathe…" I told myself.

"Promise me, you'll tell your story."

"Breathe… just breathe…" I told myself.

"Promise me. God damn it, promise me!"

"Two, three, five, seven, eleven, thirteen, seventeen…"

"If you don't promise me, I can't… you must promise me."

"I promise." The darkness took me in, flooded my senses with nothingness. The abyss wrapped me in a blanket, swaddled in the night. The sensation of falling without the rush collapsed my stomach. My equilibrium started to play tricks with my senses.

Twisting, turning, falling. Falling into dark.

"Wake up."

"I am awake." I said. "Who are you?"

"I am you. How many times have I told you that?"

"I'm so confused," I said.

*"You have no idea **what** you are, do you?"*

"I guess not," I answered.

"What I'm about to show you is going to be hard to believe so I need you to be prepared."

"Do I have a choice?" I asked.

"There is always a choice to be had, you even have the choice to choose it."

"I don't even know what that means," I muttered.

"It means, I can be here if you want me to be. I can be gone if you don't. I'll never leave you, but I can leave you be. It's your choice."

"I don't feel like I have many choices. Everything has already been planned and set into motion for me," I said to myself. "This whole life has already happened, I'm just watching it unfold."

"I don't think you're as confused as you think. I'm going to show you, from the beginning, where everything went wrong. These memories are your memories. They are my memories. Are you ready?"

"Yes. I'm ready."

PART V

DEJA VU

CHAPTER 38

IN THE BEGINNING

"Be good." My mom reached across and opened my door for me, effectively shoving me out of the car and into the world. "I'll be waiting right here when you're done."

I took a step away from the door and pushed its mass closed behind me, offering a grunt of acknowledgement in my mother's direction. The passenger window magically lowered behind me as I stood in the grass watching the rain soaked blades wet the top of my Converse. "Go on inside, I can't leave until I know you made it in ok. I love you."

Without looking back over my shoulder, I walked through the gate and up the sidewalk to the porch. The front door was unlocked. It was always unlocked. It seemed wrong to enter without knocking but I did just that time and time again. I know it was an office, but the façade of the ranch home still made me feel like there was a hidden protocol I was refusing to follow. I turned the metal screen door handle and stepped inside. I could hear my mom's Lincoln pull away from the curb before the screen door closed behind me. The heat outside was miniscule and definitely did not warrant the chilled atmosphere in the lobby. A window air conditioning unit hummed and blew red ribbons horizontally into the room as if it were still on display at the hardware store.

I walked across the hardwood floor and took my usual place in the chair opposite the receptionist. The smell of lilacs was so potent it bordered on toxic. I was forced to take a breath, hold it and then release through pursed lips. A candle store going up in flames would have been easier to stomach than this waiting room. My eyes started to water, which could be misconstrued as tears, pissing me off instantly. Stupid flowers. I swung my legs freely in the solitary chair while my hands tapped out a beat on the dark stained oak armrests. The window to my left was covered in matching dark wood blinds, turned slightly toward the ceiling. A broken rainbow of sunlight peeked through and danced on the contrasting hardwood floor as clouds slowly made their way beyond the confines of my holding cell. With a click, the air conditioning unit stopped and the red ribbons fell lifeless against the front.

I looked up at the receptionist, Christie, busy typing away loudly behind the raised counter. The whir and hum of the electric typewriter competed with the soft woodwinds floating down out of the ceiling tile speakers. Her typing echoed through the office, breaking the monotony with each fevered stroke. I counted the key clicks and tried to imagine the words as they inked the page. In my head she was writing a letter to the editor of the daily newspaper about how furious she was with the current state of affairs surrounding the shade of red illuminating from the city's stoplights. The red light, according to a study she'd read in a medical journal, actually incited violence toward women. She was requesting the stoplights be changed to blue/yellow/white instead of red/yellow/green in order to cut down on the ever-growing problem of domestic abuse. Christie looked up and smiled. I looked down and blushed.

This wasn't the first office I'd been to and I doubted it would be the last. Recently, my parents had decided to the fact that their son did not think the way other people think.

My pediatrician had pointed out that my problems were not being corrected by conventional means; it was time to move on to a more unconventional approach.

Against everything they'd ever told themselves, I was turned over to the educated assistance of a therapist. I was actively a member of the community of lost souls, spilling their darkest innermost thoughts to a trained professional. Soon I'd be asked, "How does that make you feel?" and prompted "let's explore this deeper," while I basically worked through my own issues. The psychiatrist was nothing more than a mediator between my body and my mind. Once again, someone else would be taking credit for me solving my own problems.

"How old are you?" the receptionist asked. I ignored her as long as I could get away with it. It wasn't that I was being rude, it was just that I was trying to avoid the impure thoughts that ran through my head at night thinking back to her smile, her glasses, her ponytail bouncing as she typed away on the humming typewriter deep in her personal memoirs about how she was obsessed with stealing a young boy's virginity and welcoming him to manhood by way of her seductive charm and heavenly perfume... or that's how I'd imagine it later when I told The Shadow Man about the afternoon's events. Did I mention I was sexually advanced and frustrated as an eight year old?

"Oh fine, ignore me. You must be the strong silent type." This time I looked up. Sure enough, Christie peeked over the top of her horn-rimmed glasses with perfect hazel eyes, a smile and a tiny pointed chin propped up on two slender hands. I smiled then remembered she was waiting for an answer so I held up both hands, in an effort to display ten outstretched fingers. Okay, I lied. Not a big lie, but blinded by my hormone riddled adolescence I assumed I had a better shot with her If she at least thought I'd breached into the world of double digits.

She tilted her head and smirked, obviously wooed by my prowess. I mentally patted myself on the back for the last minute decision to bump myself to ten. The more I thought about it, ten is a perfectly acceptable, well-rounded number; a perfect ten, base ten, the metric system, ten fold... I smiled and let it reach all the way to my eyes. When I wanted to, I could be charming as hell. When I needed to, I could be ruthlessly adorable. I had so many women wrapped around my fingers with a flash of deep brown eyes and a toothy smile that I could get away with damn near anything. I winked.

Her smirk relaxed until her jaw dropped between her

palms and her eyes showed more white than hazel. Her astonished look confirmed I'd surprised her. My smile grew wider. Her eyes grew to match. "Ten?" she asked. I nodded vigorously. She sat back in her chair and crossed her arms over her chest. Her mouth no longer agape, a thin-lipped smile appeared as she slowly shook her head back and forth. "You're trouble, mister." I continued to nod vigorously.

With a "tsk tsk tsk" and a huff, she giggled to herself and returned to her typewriter. I had at least left an impression. I returned to the task of swinging my legs back and forth below the chair in an attempt to will myself to the playground at school where I should have been at that given moment. I listened closely to the sound of a car speeding up and shifting gears as it attempted to make a yellow light. I looked up and watched the smooth red door across from me open gracefully as the screech of tires outside let me know the light had changed to red sooner rather than later.

"Travis, she's ready for you now." I took a deep breath and hopped down off of the chair. I grabbed my coat and walked toward the open door. The woman I approached was new so I took a moment to take her all in. I walked a little slower and noticed I could see the top edge of her stocking peeking out from under the hem of her skirt. I sped up, realizing that I was staring. As I grew nearer, I looked up and saw the expression on her face. No smile, she'd caught me looking.

I offered a simple yet innocent, "Hi."

That must have done it. "Hi. I'm sure you know where you're going by now, huh?" She smiled.

"Yep," I answered with delight as I turned on my heel and walked backwards down the hall, making sure she saw the smile on my face before she entered her own office.

I turned around just as I reached the end of the hall. Face to face with the door that led me to salvation, I brushed my hair with my hands and adjusted my shirt. I wasn't trying to impress; it was nervous behavior. I hated going into this office. The questions always seemed to point the finger back at me. I felt as if I had to defend myself the entire time I was on the couch. I did not like being the object of attention either. Once I went through those doors, I became a guinea pig.

I reached for the handle and hesitated. I checked my hair once more and pulled my shirt out only to tuck it back in.

Before I could finish, the door opened in front of me. There she stood, waiting.

"I was beginning to get worried that you weren't going to come have lunch with me," she said as she looked down on me from atop her menacing height. Her voice whispered the words with annoyance shrouded by the caress of compassion. I was convinced. She wanted me to break.

CHAPTER 39

THROUGH THICK AND THIN

She moved aside and allowed me entrance to her inner sanctum. I stepped lively and took my place on the couch per my weekly routine. She shut the door and strode around her desk, picking up a brown paper sack on her way to sit beside me on the couch. I watched as she opened the bag and placed its contents on two paper plates, evenly distributed despite our obvious difference in mass and apparent hunger. "Have you forgotten my rules so soon?" she asked. Without a word of protest, I jumped up off of the couch and ran to the sink in her private bathroom. Stretching on extended toes, I let loose the hot water and proceeded to wash my hands thoroughly.

Turning on the faucet was much easier than turning it off so I resorted to teetering on the edge of the sink abreast the fulcrum of my favorite nylon Star Wars belt.

Upon reentering her office, I noticed her watching me. She always watched me with evaluating eyes. I could feel her comparing my every movement and response, looking for a meaning that may or may not even be there. I could feel her plotting. "You look as if you're deep in something cerebral. A penny for your thoughts?" she asked. I slowed my walk, purposely modifying my pace just to see her reaction. What would it mean if I walked bow legged? How about backwards? What if I skipped across the room and took a shit on the carpet? How would her textbooks define that?

"A penny huh? With what my mom is paying you, that's all you can afford to spare?" Damn, I was clever. She huffed and handed me my plate. "Thank you," I continued politely. She smiled, pleased with my manners. The first fifteen minutes were always spent over a plate of kettle-cooked potato chips, peanut butter sandwiches, an apple and a carton of chocolate milk.

We ate in silence. I'd make sure to check her progress out of my peripheral after every bite. I didn't want her to think I was beginning to like her or that I was letting my guard down just because she was playing on my desire for food.

"Is it good?" she asked. I nodded and mumbled an agreement through a mouthful of bread and sticky peanut butter. At first I would eat the sandwich, then the apple and finish with the chips. After a while, I thought it would be interesting to mix things up a bit. I'd eat everything backwards for a few weeks. Then sometimes I'd eat a little of each or in no particular order whatsoever, sporadic and without pattern. Anything I could do to deliberately throw off her evaluation of my current mental state, I found devilishly fun.

"Would you like something different for a change?" she asked as I popped the last kettle chip into my mouth. "…for next week I mean."

I crunched the chip slowly, and then turned to face her, "How about steak?"

She laughed then retorted, "Peanut butter it is." Ok, maybe I did like her a little bit. "Did you bring your sleep journal?" she asked as she gathered our discarded plates and napkins. I reached into my bag and pulled out the ragged red notebook I'd been writing in every morning for the last few months.

"How have you been sleeping?" she asked. She always asked. I had finally resorted to a simple look that answered the question for me. "I'll take that as no changes." She picked up the red notebook lying beside me on the couch and began to flip through to the last entry.

"I fell asleep while I was getting my hair cut. He slipped and nicked my scalp when my head nodded forward. Wanna see?" I bent over and started to inspect my scalp with my fingers, looking for the tender scab that a pair of razor sharp scissors had created.

"Did you have to have stitches?" she seemed mildly concerned, more skeptical than sympathetic. I was silent for a few moments more before I located the rough edge of the wound with my fingertip. I winced as I scratched the cut accidentally. She leaned over, observed the scab and sat back with a low whistle. "What day was that?"

I smoothed my hair back to a presentable part and answered, "Tuesday I think. No, Monday."

She laughed again. "This is what I want you to write in your journal." She said it with a smile, but emphasized her every word with a finger tap to the beaten red cover.

I sat silently, pondering the creases in the back of my thumb, pretending to ignore her as she flipped through my journal. Some weeks I wrote more, some less. A couple months back I'd written nonsense just to see if she was reading it or not. I first added a sentence in the middle of a dream recollection to see if she'd say anything or give away whether or not she saw it. "I hope she isn't reading this because if she is she'll know that I dream about her without clothes on and I made this all up just to have an excuse to come see her." She'd never acknowledged the sentence so the next week I tried it again, this time more risqué.

Week after week, I'd ramped up the intensity and severity of my asides until she'd finally put the spiral notebook down and sighed. She had rubbed her forehead with her left hand, kneading her temples between her thumb and middle finger. "Yes, I do read it all, my dear. Each week I read every word. You can stop with the vulgarity now. *Please*. At first it was cute, but now it's just a bit much. Ok?" I had sat in silence contemplating the creases on the back of my thumb much like I was doing now.

Since that day, my journal had been a chore. I'd kept my

entries brief, concise and free of discussion regarding the seam up the back of her stockings. Today, the journal was simple and boring. It didn't take her long to return the notebook to the couch and start the actual discussion with a new question, "What do you want to get out of these sessions?"

What do I want to get out of these sessions? She'd never before presented me with a question so obligatory. Was she frustrated at my progress? "Why?" I asked.

She smiled and stood to lean back against the edge of her desk. "I just want to take a moment and reconsider why it is we're here and what you want to get out of all of this." She gestured around the room with her hands then crossed her arms. Her eyebrows rose to disappear beneath her bangs emphasizing the validity of her quandary.

"I want to be able to sleep like a normal kid?" I asked, because I still wasn't sure of the point to this new line of questioning.

"You, my dear, are not a 'normal kid' and the one thing I've picked up on in here, spending so much quality time together, is that your lack of sleep bothers everyone else much more so than it does you. I ask again, what do you want to get out of these sessions?"

I looked down at a white patch of worn denim on the knee of my jeans. "I want to stop thinking about the universe."

She didn't say a word, simply stood and walked back over to my side. "I think I may be at my end here. Unless you feel like you are still making progress, I can no longer continue these sessions in good conscious without you being aware of what I see as my current limitations. The truth is, I feel like we're spinning our wheels." I looked up then. She was perched on the arm of the couch, looking down at me through pity filled eyes I'd never seen the likes of before.

"I do feel like we're making progress. I promise!" I blurted out, pleading now.

"I think you are simply getting more used to the situation instead of turning it positive. I'm afraid that if I continue with you, I'm stealing the opportunity from you to grow with another, more capable therapist."

I looked at her without the need to manipulate because my honesty ran down my face in swells. "You're giving up on me too."

"No, I am not giving up on you." She placed her palm on the top of my head. "I don't want you to ever feel like anyone has given up on you." She ruffled my hair, then quickly removed her hand and walked back over to her chair. She hesitated a moment then turned back toward me. "No matter what happens, Travis, I don't want you to ever think I've given up on you. In all honesty, I've done quite the opposite."

I smiled and replied, "Thank you Katherine." She nodded, smiled and turned her back to retrieve some unseen necessity from her purse.

The rest of the session we talked about Atari. She'd purchased a 2600 for her son and was instantly addicted herself. These were the sessions where I left in good spirits. What I wanted most was answers but I was intelligent and self aware enough to recognize my fears as irrational. Seeking answers was not the key and I realized it as such. What I needed was acceptance. I needed someone to believe me. Katherine did just that...

CHAPTER 40

MAKING WAVES

My sessions continued as expected. Each week we would eat our pre-discussion snack, discuss my sleep for the previous week, check my red journal and finally dig a little into what had happened since we'd last met.

Then she decided to ask the hard question. "What frightens you, Travis?" I looked at her, confused, because I was just about to tell her the story of a scuffle that took place in the coatroom the day before over who had the most Star Wars action figures.

"What do you mean?" I asked. I knew full well what she

meant. I was stalling.

"What frightens you? What causes the panic attacks? This is the whole reason we're here after all, isn't it?"

I opened my mouth then closed it again. "I thought we were here because I can't sleep." It sounded intelligent.

"You're stalling." She was more observant than I had anticipated. I chose to sit quietly rather than answer the question. She chose to observe rather than press. "Yes, we are here because you are not sleeping, but I believe we are both aware of *why* you are not sleeping. It's the elephant in the room. I think it's time we start to discuss it. Don't you?" I opened my mouth then closed it again before looking down at my faded jeans.

The session ended that day in silence. She was right. I was stalling. It wasn't that I didn't want to explore my fears; it was that explaining them seemed so cliché. I'd run through them in my head so much that running through them out loud was only going to make me seem crazier than I already was. There was nothing I could say that I could ever imagine being productive or doing anything other than making me more confused or getting me fit for a straight jacket.

"How did your session with Dr Hill go?" My mother asked when I'd gotten into the car.

"Her name's Katherine. I don't call her Dr Hill. I think she perceives the formality as a barrier between me thinking of her as an adult and me thinking of her as a friend."

"*Sooo...* how did your session with *Katherine* go?" My mother asked as she pulled the Lincoln away from the curb and through the yellow light beyond.

That night, I'd sprawled out in my bed and conversed with the shadows. When the questions became too heavy for my head to bear, I entered my own private world and left this one far behind.

The next morning, I looked at my sleep journal and kept walking to the bathroom. I did not want to write in the journal. I hated that worn red spiral notebook.

That night, after spending a few hours chasing the creatures that inhabited the corners of my room with my frantic sideways glances, I began to demonize the journal. What did I want out of the sessions with Katherine? I wanted to be free of the anchors that reminded me of my issues. That notebook was an anchor. It had to be destroyed in order for my body to find the rest that it needed. It was my own personal voodoo doll.

I raced to the kitchen and threw it in the trashcan and snuck back to bed more careful on the return than I was on the emprise. I curled up in bed with a smile. I felt better already.

But I didn't at all. An hour later, I realized that the voodoo magic contained in the cheap red notebook was much more powerful than could be countered by discarding it in a kitchen wastebasket. It must be destroyed by fire; burned at the stake like a Salem witch being absolved of her sins.

I picked up my pants and socks, carrying them with me down the stairs and into the kitchen. I pulled the trashcan out from under the counter and peered inside. It looked back at me. Smug. It didn't know I'd just figured out how to destroy it. I reached in, rolled it up and heading out the back door as cautious as possible toward the garage.

Twenty minutes later I was back in my bed feeling relieved. I would get back up before everyone else and thoroughly clean the garage. I hoped the black mark on the concrete where I'd burned the notebook would be gone by morning but deep down I knew it would not. I knew that the actions I had just taken would end with me in trouble. Regardless, they were necessary. The journal needed to be destroyed.

The next morning I sat up in a haze. I knew I had done something the night before, but no matter how hard I tried I couldn't pinpoint the activities. I reached for my sleep journal on the bedside table. Gone. It all flooded back. There was no point in trying to forge or replace the sleep journal. What was done was done.

My mother pulled up in front of the converted ranch. "I'll be back in an hour." She reached over unlatched my door and kissed me on the cheek in a mock effort to expedite my departure. "I love you," she said as I pushed the massive steel door shut behind me. I strode slowly away from my mom's bright red metallic Lincoln Continental and reluctantly closed the gap between the screen door and myself.

I turned the knob without a knock as my routine had been for weeks. The smell of roses was so potent it bordered on toxic. I was forced to take a breath, hold it and then release through pursed lips. A tire factory going up in flames would have been easier to stomach than this waiting room. My eyes started to water, which could be misconstrued as tears, pissing me off instantly. Stupid flowers.

"Hello, Travis. Have a seat, Katherine will be with you in a moment." Normally I would have been excited to see the attractive smile Christie always wore, but lately I was unable to muster even a "hello" in return. I swung my legs freely in the solitary chair while my hands tapped out a beat on the dark stained oak armrests. Once again I found myself staring off into nothing hoping for a piece of space debris to come flying down from the cosmos, crash through the roof and land square on my head.

"Travis?" The door opened and I was ushered back down the familiar hall to Katherine's office where she stood waiting in the doorway.

"Where's your sleep journal?" she asked as I slipped by under her arm. She'd obviously noticed my empty hands.

"It's gone." I took the same seat I'd taken for as long as I could remember.

"What do you mean it's gone?" She asked, closing the door behind her.

"Gone. Just gone." I said, not wanting to admit what had happened. What was done was done. My best bet now was to change the subject, "*So...* peanut butter sandwiches?"

"No sandwiches today, I'm afraid. Today, we bite the bullet and start talking about your fears." She walked over to her desk, grabbed her chair and wheeled it around to face me on the couch. She picked up one end of the coffee table and pivoted it 90° to give her an unobstructed view. Moving the giant red coffee table also blocked my exit. I was trapped. Five minutes passed in silence. I looked down at the knees of my jeans. Focusing on the crisscross pattern of threads worn bare by childhood rambunctiousness kept my brain in brighter places.

"If you're not ready to talk about any of this, we can just sit here. I'm not opposed to it." Five minutes more passed in silence.

"I really think getting it out of your head is going to do more good than you can imagine." Five more minutes passed in silence.

"Do you know what your fear is called?" she asked. I ventured an upward glance in her direction. "It's called

Apeirophobia. It's the fear of infinite things. Did you know it was called that?" Five minutes more passed in silence.

"It's really more common than you think..." she said.

"How do you fix it?" I interrupted...

Katherine smiled. "We talk about it first. That won't fix it, but it will bring the real problem to the surface." She stared hard at my face, searching for her own answers. "Do you believe in God?" she asked after a moment's hesitation.

I tilted my head and replied, "Do you?"

She sat for a moment, and then answered honestly, "Yes, I believe I do. There has to be a greater power than us. That's just how I feel. It doesn't make it the correct answer but it does make it *my* answer."

I looked back down at my jeans; "There's no point to any of this then."

She could hear the defeat in my voice and immediately replied, "Why would you say that, Travis?"

I looked back up into her face, "If you believe in God, you can't begin to understand what it is I go through. When you look into the night sky, you already have the answer. Albeit an irrational and stupid answer based on myth and outdated folklore, but an answer in every other connotation of the definition. It isn't the *correct* answer, but it does make it *your* answer."...

"You think that my beliefs in God keep me from having an objective outlook on your fears?" Katherine asked, obviously taken aback by my inference.

"Yes, in a nutshell." I said as a matter of fact.

"We're discussing *your* beliefs not my own," she rescinded.

"No, what I'm saying is that if you have the ability to close off your mind and accept ridiculous notions like God and the Bible, then you're not intelligent enough to see the forest for the trees." I was getting irritated. "Had I known you were this stupid, we could have saved a lot of peanut butter sandwiches and I could have been spending my Wednesday afternoons at home playing Pitfall. The next thing you'll tell me is that you believe in time travel too."

"That is an incredibly rude thing to say, but I'll overlook it.

You are simply putting up walls because you are afraid of the question. This is a defense mechanism and I will not allow your childish behavior to ruin our session." She took a breath and wiped her hands on her skirt as if she were dusting off the argument. "Now, what did you say about time travel? Why would you ever associate a belief in God with time travel? Please explain."

"Both are ridiculous fantasies." I closed my eyes and hoped for that space debris to fall through the tile ceiling at any moment.

"Why?" she asked.

"Time travel is a ridiculous fantasy because if it were to ever be possible, at any point in the future, somehow, somewhere, somewhen, someone would have traveled back in time to say hello and brag about their time machine. The only plausible explanation is that a) it is science fiction and will never be possible or b) the world ends before it is invented."

"That doesn't answer why you would associate time travel with a belief in God," she pointed out.

"Clearly it does. Much like religion, time travel is a crutch created by people to allow them to sleep at night. Some people need to think that that there's something out there after this life and that everything happens for a reason so they created 'God' the same way people who want more than anything the opportunity to go back and fix something they've done or not done force themselves to believe in time travel one day being invented so they can come back to where they messed up..."

Katherine interrupted my diatribe. "Stop, stop, stop. Hold on, mister. You are stalling and trying to change the subject. Why do you find it so difficult to believe in God?"

I stood from the couch and climbed over the coffee table. "Don't get up, I'll show myself out." Katherine watched as I walked to the door and opened it. I hesitated for a moment trying to decide whether it was a good idea to slam it behind me or leave it open. She never moved from her chair as I strode back down the hall toward the waiting room, the door wide open behind me.

My mother was not near as excited at my early dismissal from therapy as I had expected her to be. "You are going to march right back in there and apologize to Katherine. Then you're gonna sit your happy ass down and listen to what she has to say." My mother, the pragmatist.

"But mom, she doesn't talk. She just listens. I talk to myself all. The. Time. This is just a waste of your money." I pleaded the financial angle knowing my mother's partiality toward the pinched penny.

"Don't make me drag you back in there kicking and screaming because, trust me, I will." My mother, the disciplinarian.

I went back inside, never said a word to Christie and simply walked back down the hallway. I waited outside her door for nearly a full minute before I knocked.

Katherine opened the door and allowed me to pass back into her office. "How have you been?" she asked, trying to get me to smile.

"Fine. It's not like I can go anywhere." I walked over and took my seat back on the couch. After I had left, Katherine had put the office back to its normal setting. I stared at the coffee table.

"Let's talk more about the religious implications into your fear," she suggested.

"Let's not and say we did," I counter offered.

She forced a laugh then continued, "What about time travel? Why would you compare time travel to religious beliefs? That seemed very odd."

I looked at her, trying to decide the best way to continue. "Do you believe in time travel?" I asked.

"I've never really thought about it," she answered honestly.

"If time travel was going to exist at any point in our future, then it would exist throughout our past. Looking infinitely into the future of possibilities, thinking that we'd eventually one day develop the technology and know-how seems viable."

"Then why don't you believe in it?" she interrupted.

"Because under the same logic, it would also make zero sense to assume that, looking *infinitely* into the future of mankind, accepting that time travel would *one day* be invented yet being ok with no one ever coming back to spill the beans. Somewhere, sometime, someone would have come back to our present and said, 'hey, look at my giant

penis shaped time machine! I'm the coolest man alive!'
That hasn't happened, therefore time travel is moot."

"That is a ridiculous argument coming from someone as intelligent as you." Katherine smiled, hoping we'd worked past the religion debacle.

"Either that or the world ends soon like I said before. Maybe that's why the technology for time travel will never be invented. Actually, that's a much more likely scenario, what with the continued arms race and nuclear weapons in the hands of every nutjob with a private military." I looked back down at the back of my thumb.

"Do you think the world is going to end?" she asked.

"What does your God say about that?" I retorted.

"That would be a pointless discussion now wouldn't it?" she asked with a stern voice.

"Not near as pointless as your belief in an imaginary all powerful deity perched above the clouds." She did not see the humor.

"Belittling someone's belief is very rude, young man." Katherine sat rigid, staring directly at me. I'd found her button. Deep inside I knew it was wrong to press, but I just couldn't help it.

"I'm not belittling your belief. I'm simply pointing out that I was mistaken." I tried my best to contain the smile, hoping she'd take the bait.

"Mistaken about what?" she asked.

"I thought you were my equal. Apparently I was mistaken. There is definitely no point in discussing this further because you're obviously incapable of..." She stood up before I could complete my sentence and approached her desk. "...incapable of seeing what I have to say as anything other than nonsense and I, the like, in turn."

She pressed down on the intercom button, "Christie, can you get Travis's mother on the phone? We are going to cut today's session a bit short today."

Over the intercom, the voice crackled a reply, "I'll send her back. She's sitting out in the lobby waiting."

CHAPTER 41

GIVING UP

The look on Katherine's face shifted to dismay, then quickly returned to business, "Thank you, send her in." She moved over to the door, and opened it half way, peered out down the hall, then returned to her desk to shuffle papers and reorganize briefly.

As my mom reached the doorway, Katherine clasped her hands in front of her and smiled wide. "Knock, knock?" my mother called shyly before she crossed the threshold into my realm.

"Come in, come in." Katherine stood and met my mom as

she made her way across the carpet toward the empty chair next to the couch. "So nice to see you, again... um...." Her words slowed and trailed off before my mother could interject.

"Judy. How is Travis doing? Is everything ok?" Katherine sighed and went back to her perch behind the desk. The picturesque element of authority behind the oversized piece of solid oak screamed superiority complex. Hopefully I'd remember that so I could call her on it sometime down the road.

"I think we may be at a crossroads here. I've done everything within my power to help your son work through his crippling fears. I've reached a point where, without his full cooperation, proceeding further is pointless. I'm looking for help on your part to see if we can get him back on track." She offered a palm out in my direction to emphasize what she was establishing as 'the problem'.

"What exactly is he doing? Or not doing, rather?" My mother asked while staring holes through my flesh with laser eyes. I gave her my best, most innocent look of "What? I'm the victim here."

Katherine turned her gaze upon me as well, "He's not

doing anything that isn't expected. He feels threatened and is establishing boundaries. What I'm trying to explain is I think *he* may have decided that I'm unable to help him further. If he's not willing to allow me in, we are just spinning our wheels here and wasting mom and dad's money. I cannot, in good conscience, continue treating your son without bringing this to your attention. I hope this hasn't discouraged you, I'm really only looking for some parental assistance on your part to make sure he keeps his sleep journal in tact and that when he does attend our sessions each week, he comes well rested and ready to make a genuine effort to find the answers you both seek."

Katherine smiled warmly, allowing the sincerity to reach all the way up to her eyes. She waited patiently for a response from my mother who was still focused intently on me. I watched as my mom's rage filled eyes narrowed and the thin line between her lips started to curl on the far outer edge. She turned her piercing stare from me back to the waiting woman. Upon seeing the same expression I'd just witnessed, Katherine's smile faltered. "You hope he comes *well rested?* Do you even know why I'm bringing him here?" Katherine started to interrupt, but my mother simply spoke over her stammering interjection. "This sounds more like an attack on my parenting than a cry for help. Or is this simply you throwing your hands in the air in defeat, using my son as the scapegoat?"

She stood and turned back to me. "Are you ready?" she asked. I stood and started for the door. "I'd like you to think about what I said. When I bring him back next week, I'll come in with him. You can let me know at that time whether or not you feel you've reached your professional limit. I understand he may be difficult to deal with at times. This is why he is here, after all." My mother followed behind me, except she opted to shut the door to Katherine's office behind her, effectively cutting off the rebuttal that had already begun.

The following week, I found myself sitting in Katherine's office next to my mother, across from a much smaller woman no longer smiling behind a big oversized desk. Katherine had traded in the show of superiority for a servant's persona. I wondered if her contrived tactics were performed on purpose or simple sad cliché. "I have discussed with another colleague your son's case... I say 'case' because I feel that the problems he is facing are not as easily fixed as finding a suppressed memory or facing a fear. This is where everyone who has seen him before has come to an end I am assuming?"

My mother nodded, "More or less."

Katherine stood and walked around to her desk. "That being said, I'd like to present you with another possibility. The colleague I referred Travis to is currently working on a research study for gifted children at the University. The person in charge is a brilliant therapist who specializes in cases similar to your son's. We spoke over the phone and think that Travis would make an excellent addition to the study. The theory is to reprogram the brain to ignore the fear and questions that bother him through hypnosis."

Katherine took a drink of water and continued, "I can already tell that you're skeptical, but please hear me out. The nature of Travis's fear lies in the unknown. It's difficult, to say the least, for someone to face and accept a fear when the fear itself is of…" She paused for dramatic effect, "…the unknown. I think this is the best possible option for Travis. It's your decision, as always. Also, I should point out, that if you do accept the offer and sign a waiver allowing Travis to be used as part of a case study for other children facing the same or similar problems, the therapy sessions will be free of charge until the study has completed. Please mull it over and let me know as soon as possible so I can call Dr Schicksal."

My mother listened to Katherine's spiel with a perfect poker face. When she was finally finished talking, my mother simply stood, patted me on the shoulder and crossed to the door. She paused and spoke over her shoulder. "We'll let you know in the next day or so how we plan to proceed." My mother straightened and headed down the hall, expecting me to follow.

Follow I did, pausing momentarily in the doorway to speak over my shoulder as well, "I told you that you'd eventually give up on me. Everyone gives up on me." I walked out and pulled the door shut behind me effectively cutting off the rebuttal that had already begun.

CHAPTER 42

A NEW CHAPTER

"I can't believe the nerve of that woman!" my mother said to my father. I was sitting on the top step, listening to their conversation as it floated up the stairs from the kitchen below. "Can you believe she blamed *me*?"

"Actually, it sounds like she blamed your son." My father, the voice of reason.

"You weren't there. You didn't hear the tone in her voice."

"Sometimes you can be such a woman. You've felt this was your fault from the very beginning," my father's voice approached so I quickly slid back against the wall away from the rail, "Nothing the Doctor said is going to change that." My father left the kitchen and strode through the dining room below.

"What do I tell her then? Are we going to try this other Doctor?" She followed him through the house, their voices trailing off once they closed their bedroom door.

The following morning, my parents sat me down at the kitchen booth. My mother fed my sister in her highchair as my dad stood and leaned against the counter. "We discussed your therapy last night at length," he said.

"I heard." I took a bite of toast.

They exchanged a disgruntled look then my mother continued, "Do you think seeing the new Doctor is a good idea? I mean, do you want to give it a try?"

"I don't know." I took another bite of toast.

"That's not an answer, son." My dad walked over and sat down in the booth beside me, grabbing my last piece of toast before I could. "We're not moving forward unless you are willing to give it your best shot at success." He took a bite and smiled. He was always stealing my food. It was our own little game.

"Yes, I think we should give it a shot." I reached for my chocolate milk. "What do I have to lose?"

"That's what I wanted to hear." My dad put down the half eaten piece of toast and walked over to the phone. "We just needed to hear it from you before we made the call."

As my dad dialed the number on the business card we were handed the day before, my mother cooed at my sister and shoveled another bite into her open mouth. "I *am* hopeful this time. I think this is going to finally help you." She looked over at me before reaching for her own coffee. "I love you. I just want to make sure we're doing what's best for you."

The following day, I was sitting in the back of my dad's Suburban next to my sister, driving south to the University. My parents were both asked to attend the first session to establish where and how the treatment should begin. My mom turned around in her seat and handed a pacifier to my sister while offering me the same in the form of motherly advice, "You'll be fine. Nothing to worry about.

You should be an old pro at this point anyway, right?"

I wasn't worried. I wasn't nervous. If anything, I felt calm and at ease. A feeling of déjà vu washed over me as we walked through the giant automatic doors into the psychology building. I stood beside my mother and watched students of all ages walk by carrying backpacks and books. Everyone seemed so tall and oblivious. Each person was headed off in his or her own direction, intent on solving a problem or meeting a deadline. The looks on each of their faces made me feel small and insignificant.

"I think this is it," my mother pointed at a name on the brass plaque on the wall beside the elevator. "Fifth floor. Can you press the button honey?" she asked. I reached for the up arrow at eye level as another pair of women walked behind me carrying a box of fresh pizza, discussing sitcom television. I released the button and turned to watch them sway down the hall and turn a corner out of sight.

"Eyes forward, Casanova." My dad chuckled and entered the elevator as the doors spread and invited us inside.

"We're here to see Dr Schicksal." My mother shifted my sister to her opposite hip.

"What's the first name?" the receptionist asked.

"Travis," my father offered as he hugged me closer to his leg.

She looked down her list, and then picked up the phone. "Please let Dr Schicksal know that the new subject has arrived." She hung the phone up and pointed at a row of plastic chairs on the far wall. "If you'll have a seat over there, the Doctor will be right out."

Forty-five minutes later, the large double doors we'd previously entered opened up and a large mechanical wheelchair slowly wheeled through powered only by a straw and the distorted figure that looked nothing like any therapist I'd ever encountered. "Hell oh. I am Doc ter Shik Sal. It is my plezsh er to meet you." The electronic voice electrified the room from a speaker on the armrest of the chair.

CHAPTER 43

ACCEPTED

No one moved. My father looked like a deer in headlights. The appearance of Dr Schicksal was more than unexpected. It was downright disturbing. The Doctor obviously recognized our discomfort. The wheelchair rotated until it was aimed directly at me. "You must be Ter-ah-vis."

"Yes," I said. "This is my mom and dad and my little sister. It's a pleasure to meet you as well." I approached the wheelchair with my hand stretched out to shake the Doctor's but quickly dropped it when I realized there were no hands to shake.

"Dr Schicksal is in a bit of hurry today so I was asked to make sure you had the opportunity to meet." A man in his mid twenties standing behind the wheelchair spoke. I hadn't noticed him standing there until that moment. The initial sight of Dr Schicksal was such a shock to the senses; everything else seemed to fade away. "Dr Schicksal's assistant, Melissa, will be with you in a moment to get the testing underway. Excuse me Doctor, we have a tight schedule to keep."

The wheelchair turned toward the man speaking. "Thank you my dear." Slowly, the wheelchair rotated back in my direction. "Sum-times I think he thinks we are mare-eed." With a huff, the man the Dr was referring to turned and headed out through the doors as they opened in just enough time to allow him to pass. "That was not what I meant when I asked him for a hand." I smiled at the Doctor, recognizing the attempt at humor.

The wheelchair backed up and started to turn. "Kath-er-in was right. You are ver-ee poh-lite. Nice to meet you." The wheelchair continued its rotation and sped off through the doors as they closed behind.

"Thank you, Dr Schicksal." My mother finally returned to life, just as the doors clicked closed. "Oh dear. I'm so embarrassed."

"What the hell was that?" my dad asked.

"That was Dr Schicksal. Really a magnificent genius, don't let the chair fool you. There's a beautiful and brilliant mind in there, it's something you have to look for, once you get past the outward shock of the obvious physical deformities and the mechanical assistance." The voice came from behind, approaching quickly astride high heels and a short gray skirt. "I'm Melissa, Dr Schicksal's assistant. Travis, you'll be coming with me. Mom and dad, if you'll follow as well, I'll show you to the waiting area." She turned and started off the way she came.

"Wait, miss? Where are we going and what is going on? I thought we were here to meet Dr Schicksal." My father followed her asking for clarification as my mother gathered our belongings including my sister and myself. "Miss? Ma'am?"

Over her shoulder she explained, "It's Melissa. Today, we need to run a few tests on Travis to make sure he qualifies for the study. It's a series of questions and a few activities similar to an IQ test but a little more involved. He'll be fine, in fact, it's actually quite fun." She turned, smiled and ushered my parents into a large room with a couch, a few recliners and a television tuned to replays from last night's football game. "If you'll wait in here, this won't take long."

She lied. Five hours later, I was reunited with my nervous and upset family. "We were so worried." My mother stood and met me at the doorway with open arms.

"Why?" I asked.

"Where were you?" she asked.

"What did they do with you that whole time?" my dad asked.

"Just games and questions and stuff. Nothing special." I walked back over to Melissa who was still standing in the doorway smiling. "Thank you. That was fun."

She knelt and pinched my cheek playfully. "Next week then?" she asked.

"Can't wait." I said as I followed her out the hall and back toward the main entrance, my parents in tow.

I had spent the entire afternoon answering question after question concerning everything from the Pythagorean theorem to Latin derivations. I'd spent an hour with a set of Legos and the simple instructions to build a time machine. There were hearing tests, an eye chart, memory recollection and even a dexterity test.

"This all seems very odd to me." My mother turned to my father, "What do you think? Are we doing the right thing?"

My father just shrugged then turned his attention to me. "It sounds like you had fun?"

"I did. Miss Melissa was with me the whole time. Dr Schicksal only came in for a moment. *'ARE YOU OH KAY?'* came out of the speaker," I exaggerated the words with my best computer voice as my mother frowned her disapproval. "Dr Schicksal asked if the tests were too much. If they were I could come back and finish another day. I told the Doc I was fine. Then I got homework."

"Homework? What kind of homework?" my mother asked.

"I have to write an essay on the quote, 'I think, therefore I am.' I'm not allowed to get any help writing it but I'm allowed to use any method I see fit to get the information.

I'm not even allowed to let you read it or proofread. I have to bring it in exactly how I have it written. He asked if I had an encyclopedia." I looked from mom to dad and back again.

"Ok, that settles it. He had fun. By tomorrow, he'll have an encyclopedia set as well." My dad stood from the kitchen table and walked out of the room, hugging my mother around the shoulder before he departed.

The next few days I wrote my first essay. Before beginning I spent several hours marveling at my very own set of used Encyclopedia Britannica. The amount of information held within amazed me. "If I read all of these books, I'd the smartest boy in the world," I vowed once the essay was complete. I'd start from the beginning and read each and every page of the set until I had compiled the full wealth of human knowledge to the annals of my brain. First I needed to look up "I think, therefore I am."

Nothing.

Next, I figured it more prudent to look up "essay" to see exactly what I was supposed to be doing in the first place. With that out of the way, it was back to the drawing board for "I think, therefore I am." Where should I begin?

I called my aunt. Both my aunt and uncle had attended college. They were the only well educated members of my family so I immediately considered them the most intelligent. Explaining to her that I was writing an essay on the quote brought about more questions than answers. "Why are you writing an essay? You shouldn't be expected to write an essay at this age. Let me speak to your mom."

"It's not for school. Do you know who said it?" I asked.

"Yes, I believe it was Friedrich Nietzsche a nineteenth century philosopher," she answered.

"Thank you! That's all I needed. Here's mom…" I handed the phone off to allow my mother to explain further as I rushed back to the stack of light tan books waiting for instruction.

Unfortunately, Friedrich Nietzsche was another dead end. He did not say, "I think, therefore I am." I spent what seemed like days cross referencing philosophers and working backward until I ended up at Bernard Williams a living moral philosopher. Williams went to great lengths to criticize Rene Descartes for his "cogito ergo sum". I already knew that "cogito" was Latin for "I think" from the battery of tests I'd taken earlier in the week. A few more minutes and the mystery was solved. I spent a few more hours reading about Descartes and "cogito ergo sum" until I felt confident enough to attempt my first essay.

The following Wednesday, my mother was sitting in the waiting room and I was back at the long white table I'd spent the weekend before, essay in hand, waiting for Melissa. I had written a full page and a half on the quote. I'd discussed its origin, the controversy, Williams, Nietzsche and it's translation. I felt very confident.

The door opened and in rolled the menacing wheelchair with Dr Schicksal nestled in the heart of the contraption. "Good after-noon Ter-ah-vis." The wheelchair came to a stop on the opposite side of the table. "Are you fry-tend?" the mechanical voice asked.

"No," I said calmly. "Everyone is different. That doesn't make you scary."

"True but my voice and my uh-peer-ents may be. I un-der-stand." The speakers crackled the answer without Dr Schicksal moving a lip.

"Maybe a little." I offered.

"Much bet-ter," the Doctor answered.

The doors opened and Melissa entered the room. She smiled brightly and proceeded to a chair sitting in the corner of the room. "How are you Travis? Were you able to complete your homework assignment?" she asked as she drug the chair next to me at the table.

"Yes ma'am." I handed her my stapled essay. I looked back at Dr Schicksal assuming they'd be impressed with my effort.

"Please, just call me Melissa. My mother is a 'ma'am', I'm just Melissa." She looked down at the paper, shook her head and tossed the paper across the table toward Dr Schicksal. "You were right. He passed. He's the only one."

"I all-red-ee knew." The wheelchair reversed away from the table and turned 180°. Melissa jumped up and ran around the table to open the door and facilitate Dr Schicksal's exit.

As the door shut behind the wheelchair, Melissa sat down across from me, picked up the essay and began to look it over again. "Can you tell me what you wrote?" she asked.

"Do you want me to read it?"

"No, not yet. First I want you to just give me an oral presentation." She looked up at me over the edge of her glasses.

"I don't know what you mean."

Again, she flashed her teeth behind a bright smile. "Just tell me what you know about the quote. Give me your impressions."

"Rene Descartes said 'cogito ergo sum' which translates to 'I think therefore I am'. The phrase is considered the building block for western knowledge. Basically it means that for someone to contemplate whether or not they exist is proof in the thought itself that they do exist."

"Ok, now what do you think it means? What does it mean to you?" she asked before flipping the paper over on the table in front of her.

"To me," I continued, "it means that no matter what, I can be sure that I am real. Everything else, even my own body and perception of reality can be false or not exist at all, but as long as I am thinking, I exist. Somehow, somewhere, somewhen I exist."

"Somewhen?" she asked.

"Yeah, somewhen. If all I know to be true is the thoughts in my head, then how do I know *when* it is?" I replied.

She leaned on the table, a smile from ear to ear. "That may be the most profound answer I've heard to that simple question. Thank you." She picked up my essay and turned it over again. "Would you like to see what you wrote?" She handed the essay back across the table.

I picked it up and started to read aloud. "I think, therefore I am was first blah blah blah blah..." I stopped reading and just stared at the page. After the first seven words the entire page was full of 'blah' after 'blah' after 'blah'. "What is this? Where's the essay I wrote?"

"That *IS* the essay you wrote. You don't remember writing 'blah blah blah blah blah'?" she asked.

"This isn't my essay." I put the paper back down in front of me and pushed it back across the table.

"Did you bring anything with you?" she asked after a moment of silence.

"No." I sat back and looked over her head at the clock beyond, watching the second hand slowly tick from mark to mark.

"Are you upset?" Melissa asked.

"No."

"You appear to be a little agitated. Can you tell me why?" she asked.

"No."

"I bet you brought me something and you don't even remember doing it." She turned in her seat to see what it was that I was staring at, then turned back to meet my gaze. "Look in your left front pocket. I bet there is a 1976 quarter in there with the letter 'M' written on it in marker." She scooted to the edge of her seat and placed her chin on the palm of her hand. Her smug smile raced across her face in anticipation of my reply.

"I didn't bring you a quarter. Why the *hell* would I bring you a quarter?" I asked, making sure to emphasize the minimal curse.

She smiled and sat back in her chair. "Well, well, well... how sure are you? Can we make a friendly wager?" She tilted her head to the side and looked at me thoughtfully. "If you do, in your pocket, have a quarter marked 'M' for Melissa, you have to tell me why it is you think you can't sleep. Deal?"

"What do I get when my pocket is empty?" I asked.

"Don't check it now!" she pointed at my hand, which was slowly moving toward the edge of the table subconsciously. "I'll take you to dinner and a movie. My treat. Your pick."

"Do you even know how old I am?" I asked, crossing my arms to keep my hand from accidentally going to my pocket prematurely.

"Old enough to say 'hell'... do we have a deal?"

"Deal." I said.

She leaned back in her chair and offered her hand, palm up, in a gesture for me to check my pocket.

I looked down at the quarter, confused. I turned it over between my fingers and saw the smeared "M" written in red marker. My breathing started to get labored, the room began to swim in a blur of heat. I looked at Melissa and saw her jump up, knocking her chair over as she put a knee up on the table reaching for me, then the blur turned to black.

CHAPTER 44

A MOMENT OF CLARITY

"Wake up."

"I am awake." I mumbled

"No, seriously, wake up."

I opened my left eye wide enough to take in my surroundings. A blurry black keyboard, millimeters from my face, slowly came into focus. I blinked once and took in the rest of my private office. I sat up, leaned back in my chair and stretched my neck in an oval, attempting to work out a few kinks. I rubbed the right side of my face, smeared with drool and wrinkled under the pressure of the remaining half of my laptop's keyboard.

"Are you awake now?"

"Yes, I am *now*." I looked around, confused. "Where…" I looked at my screen, covered in n's, m's, l's and random spaces. I started to scroll up through a dozen pages of the same looking for the beginning. "Where am I?" I found the first 'nnnllnnmmlnnn' and the few lines of a drafted Tumblr post behind it. An internet meme titled "Truthful Tuesday" with a couple of lines about my fear of infinity and insomnia cut abruptly short where my face had fallen to the keyboard mid sentence.

"What do you remember?"

"I was dreaming?" I asked.

"No, not really. Well, sort of. I was helping you remember. Do you remember?"

The dream, or whatever it was, sat in the front of my mind, as vivid as it had happened moments before. I could still smell Melissa's perfume. I looked down at my hands, turned them over and stared at my palms. I stood up on aching knees and trembling legs, checked in my front pocket for a quarter and sat back down disappointed. "Yes, I remember."

"Good. We're on the right track then."

That night, I lied in bed, trying to fall asleep, hoping for more insight into my past. When I finally woke the next morning, after a couple of hours of shuteye, there was nothing to recall. The next night, the same. And the next.

"Are you ready for more?"

"I'm trying to fall asleep." I sighed.

"If you try, I can't help."

I sat up in bed, confused. "What?"

"Stop trying so hard. If you try, I can't help."

Three more days passed without incident. It wasn't until I found myself asleep on my office floor at 2:30 in the morning, trying to get a thirty-minute nap in before an international video chat meeting, that my mind's eye took me back to my childhood.

CHAPTER 45

SUSCEPTIBLE

"Travis, are you alright?" Melissa's voice rang in my ear. "Wake up."

"I am awake." I mumbled. I opened my eyes and tried to focus on her face as she helped me upright on the floor. I felt the back of my head and came away with a small bit of blood. "What happened?"

"You saw this..." she held up a quarter "...and passed out. When you went down you hit your head on the edge of your chair." She leaned me forward and parted my hair to look at my scalp.

"Ouch!" I reached up to move her hand.

"Hold on, I see it. You have a small scratch… I think you'll be ok without stitches. Head wounds tend to bleed more than necessary. Your mom would have tanned my hide if I brought you back to her bleeding wouldn't she?" She released my head and allowed me to sit back upright. I touched my scalp again, felt the quick burn and removed my hand to see only a thin line of blood mirrored on my fingertip.

"How did you know about the quarter? Did someone put it in my pocket?" I ventured another finger to the wound.

"Stop that, it won't stop bleeding if you keep messing with it." She smacked my hand playfully and knelt in front of me on her knees, then sat down against her heels with her palms resting on her thighs. "Your report on Descartes and the quarter were a test to see how susceptible you are to hypnosis. That's part of Dr Schicksal's treatment. You don't remember the Doctor hypnotizing you at all?"

"No, I only remember a brief introduction with the doc, then you testing the crap out of me." I put my right hand in my pocket to keep from reaching back to the wound.

"That is amazing. Dr Schicksal said you were going to be the one… you were hypnotized right in the middle of the testing. The testing was meant to be a distraction. Well, we also wanted to know how intelligent you were so that you could fit within the realm of the study. You passed with flying colors on all aspects." She laughed and clapped her hands together, bringing her thumbs to her mouth before biting them through a bright smile. "Obviously," she added with two skyward eyebrows.

Melissa made good on her wager even though I had lost the bet. The following week, upon arrival at the University, I was immediately whisked away for my first date. I say "date" loosely here. Melissa took me for lunch at Casa Lapita, the only restaurant in the area without a counter to place your order. Remember, this was long before the parade of casual dining in the Midwest. This was long before Applebee's, Olive Garden or Red Lobster had made their way to every corner in the breadbasket.

After chips, salsa and tacos, Melissa treated me to a movie. "The Goonies" will always remind me of one of the best days from my childhood.

CHAPTER 46

INTERVENTION

Over the next few weeks, the dreams came every time I passed out from extreme exhaustion. If I wanted them, they never appeared. Only when I least expected it, was my head filled with the sights and sounds of my forgotten youth. Oh, and the smells... the smells were the most bizarre part. Never have I awoken from a dream and remembered specific aromas. Also, after the dreams, whenever I encounter the same smells, it triggers the experience all over again.

"What's going on with you?" Stephanie asked.

"What do you mean?"

"I don't know. It just seems like you're more stressed than usual, if that's at all possible." She pulled a chair over next to my desk and picked up my grid pad to see which sketch I was working on. "Ok, different question. Anything I can do to help?"

"Take over my Twitter account." I answered, never taking my eye off my monitor.

"Whatever," she laughed. "That's all you and Angie. I am not near funny enough for that shit."

"What did I do now?" Angie walked over from the coffee machine because hearing her name calls her like a bad urban legend, except no mirror is required.

"Don't you think Travis is more stressed than usual?" Stephanie asked over her shoulder.

"Nope. He's always an asshole." Angie took a sip of her coffee. "Who the fuck made this swill?" She sat the cup down on the edge of my desk and walked away.

"I'm being serious. What can I do to help?" Stephanie leaned in closer to Angie's discarded mug of coffee.

"Nothing. There's nothing stressing me out."

"You're not sleeping again are you?" She picked up Angie's mug, smelled it and took a cautious sip.

I pulled my hands from my keyboard and swiveled my chair to watch Stephanie as she spit the coffee back in the mug. The look on her face made me laugh.

"Fucking gross. Jesus Christ." She sat the mug back down and turned in her chair. "Fuck me, who made that pot of coffee?"

I turned back to my computer once I realized the coffee was more exciting than my stress levels. "It's not coffee," Angie called from around the corner. "It's Chai Tea or some shit. Blame Chad."

Stephanie turned back to face me. "Two things. First, don't drink the fucking coffee. Second, don't drink the fucking coffee." She stood up, replaced the chair and came back over to stand by my computer. I thrust in her direction the twice-abandoned mug of coffee, or tea... whatever it was, without looking away from my monitor. "We can tell something is going on. I wish you'd let us in. We'd be glad to help."

"I know." I looked at her and examined her face for a moment. "I know. It's just not work related. It's in my head, ya know?"

"Travis, honey, it's ALL in your head. Everything." She tapped my forehead with her finger.

I went back to the work at hand, contemplating the implications of what she'd just said. "All in my head? Maybe she's right."

"She is right."

"It's all in there, I'm just trying to remember it huh?" I asked.

"Sort of."

"This cryptic shit gets old. I just want a straight forward answer every now and again," I protested.

"Straight forward? What do you think you know about Dr Schicksal so far?"

"Just what I remember. That the doctor used hypnosis to help me accept the concept of infinity." I answered before thinking. "But, it obviously never worked."

"You're no where near ready for straight forward then."

Angie walked over and leaned against my G5 tower, staring down at me over a can of Red Bull. "She's right."

"Don't drink the fucking coffee?" I asked.

"Chai Tea... in a fucking coffee pot? I'm gonna kick Chad in his vagina for fucking with my coffee pot." She took another drink of her Red Bull and wiped the excess from the corner of her lip with her thumb. "No, that you don't seem... well... *all here.*"

"I'm fine."

"Don't give me the 'I'm fine' bullshit," she scoffed. "I've heard it before."

"I'm just working some stuff out. Really, I appreciate the concern, I just need a break." I looked up at her and once again, left my project. I made sure she knew she was keeping me from my work with the frustrated look on my face.

"Leave it. Get up." She pushed my chair back with her left foot and stepped between my computer and the chair. "Don't look at my ass, just move."

I threw my hands into the air and stumbled up and out of the way of her impending derriere. "What the fuck, Ang? These drawings have to go out today!"

"There's nothing you can do that I can't do better. I'll finish it, you go home and get some sleep." She grabbed my chair and pulled it up to the computer and started moving my mouse around as if she knew what she was doing on the project.

"God damn it. Move." I stood over her and tried to grab the mouse back from her kung fu grip. "It's not funny, you have no idea what you're doing and besides, that's my laptop, it's going with me if I'm going home."

She stopped, released the mouse and crossed her arms.

"Let us help then. Not with this, whatever it is, but with something. You're running yourself into an early grave. Everyone sees it but you."

CHAPTER 47

AN ANSWER TO THE RIDDLE

"Dr Schicksal will be in soon, Travis. In the meantime, how are you sleeping?" Melissa asked.

"Fine, I guess." I lied on the couch, watching the flickering blue and white reflections from the aquarium dance across the ceiling in the dimly lit office. For the last year, I'd been meeting Melissa and Dr Schicksal in the spare office next door to Katherine. To make things easier on my parents, Katherine had agreed to open up her practice to the study. I didn't know how many people met with the doctor, but I had the strange feeling it was only myself.

"I was looking for a more conclusive answer than 'I guess'. Can you elaborate? How many hours each night?" she asked.

"Three, maybe four."

"All at once, or broken?" she asked, writing in her notebook.

"Some nights broken, others all at once. It depends on how tired I am."

"What is keeping you awake at night? Are you still asking yourself the same questions or is something else at fault"

"I don't know, honestly, I'm just not tired. I'm not having panic attacks from my..." I didn't even like to talk about infinite space out loud anymore, "...questions... I'm really just lying in bed, awake. I don't know what to tell you."

"No, that's fine. Just be honest." She took more notes. "That's all I ask."

There was a thump at the door. "That must be Dr Schicksal." Melissa stood, folded her chair and carried it to the door. "I'll see you next week, Travis." She smiled at me then turned to open the door.

"Thanks." I said as she held the door wide. Dr Schicksal's motorized wheelchair barely fit through the wooden doorframe, bounced over the threshold and glided into the room onto the indoor-outdoor carpet. "Hello, Doc," I offered as Melissa took her leave.

"Hello, Travis." I had gotten so used to the Doc's electronic voice over the past twelve months that it no longer needed deciphering. "How have you been?"

"Good." The Doc's appearance no longer frightened me either. I wondered at times if my acceptance of the Doc's physical deformities was part of the hypnosis or if it was something else. Being in the Doc's presence seemed almost cathartic. Being with the Doc felt like home. "You told me last week that if I could answer a riddle this week I could ask a question before we started. I'm ready for my riddle." I had thought about the proposal all week. I wanted to ask the Doc what I was being told while I was under hypnosis. I really wanted to know and every time I had asked prior, I was met with resistance or outright refusal.

"I never agreed to such nonsense." The Doc swiveled the

chair back and forth to emphasize the notion. I gave my most convincing pout and huffed my exaggerated disapproval. This was all part of our game. "You drive a hard bargain young grasshopper. Ok, are you ready?"

I nodded vigorously.

"One day a father went to his three sons and told them that he would die soon. He needed to determine which one of them he would leave his fortune to. He decided to give them all a test. He said 'Go to the market my sons and purchase something that is large enough to fill my bedroom but small enough to fit in your pocket.' From this I will decide who of you is the wisest and is worthy enough to inherit my legacy.' So they all went to the market and bought something that they thought would fill the room yet was still small enough that they could fit into their pockets. Each son came back with a different item. The father told his sons to come into his bedroom one at a time and try to fill up the room with whatever they had purchased. The first son came in and put some pieces of cloth down on the floor that he had bought. He laid them end to end across the room but it barely reached the far wall. Then the second son came in and put some hay down, but there was barely enough to cover half of the floor. The third son came in and showed his father what he had purchased and how it could fill the entire room yet still fit into his pocket. The father replied 'You are truly the wisest of all, my son.' What was it that the son had showed to his father?"

I thought about the riddle for a moment. I desperately wanted to answer correctly. I opened my mouth, and then closed it.

"Do you give up? Did we discuss your penalty if you answered incorrectly?" The Doc asked.

"No, and No." I closed my eyes and ran the story through my head once more. "A match. The son lit a match, filling the room with light!"

The Doc sat motionless for a very long minute. "You surprise me again. You never cease to amaze me. Ask your question."

"How did you end up in that wheelchair?" The words leaped off my tongue before I could think about what I really wanted to say. "I'm sorry. No, I wanted to know what you were telling me while…"

"No, that's a valid question." The Doc cut me off. "I'll answer." I stopped and sat in silence. "When I was much younger, lifetimes ago, I read an intriguing book about a boy who was obsessed with infinity…"

"Is that why you started your research?" I interrupted.

"One question is all you have earned the right to ask." The Doc paused for me to apologize then continued. "The book was fascinating. I could not stop reading. It was about his life and dealing with the fear of infinite space. He was plagued with déjà vu, insomnia and a brain that would not shut off. I could not stop thinking about the book. It seemed so real to me. Shortly after I read the story, I was in a horrible car accident, much like one of the characters from the book. In the car with me was…" the Doc stopped and stared straight ahead for what felt like a lifetime.

"My family was killed. I lost everything I had ever loved in an instant. I suffered a TBI, or Traumatic Brain Injury, and lost feeling in both legs and hands. My right arm and leg were both crushed. Eventually the blood flow to all of my extremities was compromised and within a week I had both legs and arms amputated. My spine was also damaged. My windpipe was crushed. My body was broken, but my brain survived. The Traumatic Brain Injury had severe and longstanding repercussions." The doctor moved the chair closer. "All of this had been foretold by the book I'd finished days before the accident."

The Doc turned the wheelchair away from me and stared at the wood paneling lining the office wall. "I persisted and refused to die. No matter how badly I wanted to, I could not leave this world. Without having the use of my arms and legs I also lacked the ability to end my own suffering. I begged and pleaded to be euthanized without success. The damage to my brain made it difficult for me to distinguish between wrong and right, moral and immoral, good and evil. Although the brain damage I sustained inhibited my ability in some aspects it greatly increased it in other. My heightened intelligence, along with an abundance of time, gave me plenty of opportunity to devise a plan for escaping that world."

I sat in awe as the Doc reversed the wheelchair and came around to stop close by my side. "The accident also gave me the ability to influence those around me. It's not just mind tricks or carnival gags. Hypnosis became as easy as breathing through my ventilator. Experimenting one night, I discovered that once I had someone under my influence I could make them perform any task I desired."

"Like writing an essay covered in 'blah blah blah'?" I asked.

"Yes. Exactly. Now please listen before interrupting further. I decided it was better to burn than suffer endlessly. One night, I asked an orderly to cover me with floor cleaner and light me on fire. He did just as I asked, then locked the door."

I gasped in horror, but dare not interrupt.

"By the time the staff reached us, the orderly was unconscious, engulfed in flames and I was a burning pile of flesh. All the king's horses and all the king's men couldn't put the orderly back together again. But I, against all odds, survived the suicide attempt. I was unconscious, but alive nonetheless. The fire was assumed to be an attack because of my armless and legless state. Every aspect of my misfortune had been laid out for me in the final pages of the book that was now haunting my existence. I was hooked up to several machines, keeping my heart pumping and my brain working. Then... simply forgotten."

I waited, but the Doc never continued. After what seemed like a lifetime of silence I ventured a question. "How could the book have predicted the future? How could you have been forgotten?" I asked, confused by the end of the story.

"I was put into a medical coma and sat undisturbed for twenty-three years. By then, the discovery of nano technology and advancements in the medical industry provided the opportunity to wake me up. After two decades, I was brought back to a world no longer inhabited by a single person I knew or loved. All the family I had known were deceased or had moved on, wanting nothing to do with the lifeless gimp. I was abandoned and stranded in a strange place. There were many other advancements in the following decade. Nano technology erupted along with the discovery of dark matter. Much like the book I had read three days before my accident so many years before, I became obsessed with unanswered questions about the universe. I devoted my new found intelligence to something much more critical than killing myself."

"What?" I asked, forgetting not to interrupt.

Dr Schicksal moved the wheelchair beside me so that our faces were inches apart. "Time Travel," the electronic voice said slowly.

CHAPTER 48

DOCTOR DESTINY

"Time travel?" I asked with a laugh. "Why time travel?"

"What is deja vu? In French it literally means, 'already seen'. Emile Boirac, a French psychic researcher, coined the term. Déjà vu is the feeling that one has already seen or experienced the current situation before, even though the circumstances may be vague, unclear or uncertain. It's the feeling of 'I've been here and done this before.' The feeling can accompany something as simple as watching a car pass or bending over to pick up a piece of paper. It can be as unnerving as knowing every word of a conversation before it is spoken... or at least feeling as if you do. The most frequent explanation is that the experience did happen before. Picking up a piece of paper seems so random that believing the exact moment has occurred before may be a simple coincidence. Another plausible explanation is that the feeling is caused by a breakdown in the neurological system. Imagine the systems responsible for short and long term memory misfiring or firing nanoseconds apart. The result is a memory planted in the psyche before the conscious part of the brain ever receives the information and processes it, giving the illusion of past experience." I listened without choice to the Doc's methodical explanation.

"What if I were to tell you that there is no such thing as déjà vu? The feeling of déjà vu is actually your body's reaction to an event that has already occurred. We've been here many many times before. You are reliving this event, as am I, for the unknownth time. Eons may have passed, yet we are continually stuck in this bisection of time and space, destined to repeat my lifetime over and over like the needle stuck in a scratch on a vinyl record."

"I don't understand?" I asked. "This story doesn't make any sense, you don't have to tell me how you ended up this way, I'm sorry I asked." I gestured at the Doc's chair letting the fear creep into my voice a little to back the Doc off. I was not finding this entertaining at all.

"You are not an apeirophobic because there is something wrong with you, Travis. You are an apeirophobic because you know the truth. You've always known the truth. You are afraid of infinity because I have made you afraid. You are my weapon of mass destruction, my monkey wrench thrown into the gears of time. For the past year of this lifetime, I've been explaining this story to your subconscious. Someday many years in this future, you will unlock this memory. You will write the book that my past self is destined to read. I'll spend decades in a coma letting your words penetrate the deepest recesses of my brain. I'll awake and spend the rest of this lifetime trying to get back here to this very moment. Everything I've done in my life has been leading up to the summation of those events."

Dr Schicksal backed the chair up and came face to face with me, bumping the chair into the edge of the couch. I sat up feeling a bit pinned by the doctor's proximity. The electronic speaker on the wheelchair hummed, and then crackled to life. "I have a confession to make. I became obsessed with time travel because of that book. I want to bring humanity to its knees and force existence into a stutter effectively ending everything as we know it."

I stared at the Doc, my heart beginning to race. "Time travel is science fiction." I shook my head trying to grab at reality. "Otherwise people would have traveled back in time and told us about it." My explanation was lackluster at best. The words were becoming difficult to string together.

"Time travel is not science fiction my dearest Travis. It will be science fact, yet, alas, the world will never know it as we do. I, being the sole scientist to ever attempt the feat, effectively paused the timeline in the future when I first folded space back to the point of my return to the past. The future cannot move forward until the current timeline comes full circle to future. What we are doing here, in this marvelous room, is perpetuating the cycle. There will never be another time travel experiment save my own because time will never break free of this pattern as long as you and I meet."

My chest grew tight and the room began to spin.

"As you may have guessed by now, Dr Schicksal is not my real name. Do you know what Schicksal means? It means destiny. It means fate. I am sorry. This must be done. The story is no longer my own. These events have already occurred, we are merely two pawns on the path to checkmate."

My heart tried to punch a hole in my chest. I took a deep breath and steadied myself enough to speak. "Why would you tell me this? Is this part of my therapy?"

The Doc's emotionless face oozed apathy. "Because I must. When I first began experimenting with manipulating the space-time continuum the possibility of it working seemed non-existent. I was simply trying to make advances in the field. Then, I had a breakthrough and discovered the key to turning back the clock was by forgetting there was a clock at all. Time is a linear constraint that we have created as a crutch to explain what we cannot explain. Throwing that aside, I was able to fold the linear path upon itself and create an overlap between two points on the same timeline. In essence I created a loop in the continuum. Once I realized this, I knew I had to be the first to test the theory. I did not trust anyone else. I traveled across space and time to prove my theory. It wasn't until after I crossed from the point in my present to the point in the past, that I discovered the phenomenon was irreversible. I became stuck. The only way back to my present was to live through this past."

I began to have trouble breathing.

"I had forgotten my purpose. It was not intelligence and

scientific breakthroughs that had brought me back in time. It was my destiny. It was our destiny. That book from my past, from your future, had prophesized this encounter. I stopped fighting my destiny and accepted it as my fate. I knew what I had to do. I remembered that book: the book that destroyed my life. The book that led me here to you."

The sound of my surging blood filled my ears like the house was suddenly under high tide.

"Goodbye dear boy, until I see you again, please know that I am sorry to have put you through this. Someday you'll find peace and be able to sleep once again. I've grown very fond of you in this lifetime. I assume I have probably done the same in all the lifetimes past. Thank you Travis for what you will do for me. To me. Just remember, I think therefore I am. That is the only truth."

My vision blurred and black started to fill in behind the unfocussed haze that used to be Katherine's spare office.

Soon there was nothing but the cold black of outer space. My body once again floated into the abyss.

"Wake up."

"I am awake." I mumbled.

"Do you remember now?"

"Yes," I answered. "I remember."

"Do you know who I am?"

"You are me."

"I am me."

"I think, therefore I am." I pondered that notion. "This is the only truth isn't it?"

"Yes. I'm sorry, I really wanted you to break the cycle this time. I really did."

"How could I have?" I asked.

"When you were a child, you needed to overcome your fear on your own to keep the events from unfolding, leading you to Doctor Destiny. I tried to lead you, I tried to help, but you always choose to drive down this path."

"I never felt like I had a choice." I confessed.

"There was always a choice to be had, you even had the choice to choose it."

"I don't even know what that means," I muttered.

"It means, I could be here if you wanted me to be. I could have been gone if you didn't. I could never leave you, but I could have left you be. It was your choice."

"I don't feel like I ever had a choice. Everything has already been planned and set into motion for me. This whole life has already happened, I just watched it unfold." I closed my eyes and wished for quiet.

"Over the many lifetimes you've been asked to do this, your psyche retains remnants of the repetition. Over the many lifetimes those remnants have splintered your psyche. The Shadow Man is your past conscience; your guilt and obsession made whole within your mind. He plays to your fears and your unbridled drive toward satisfaction. I am your past decisions personified, staying with you to help you guide you through this life once again. If The Shadow Man is your Id, then I am your Ego. Together we have been helping you choose your path,

*kicking you back to the trail whenever you wonder off into the woods. The path is never the same. The path you've chosen **has** changed. It always changes. We need to just change it sooner rather than later. Next time."*

"Next time?" I asked.

*"Yes, next time. You will, no matter how hard you try **not to**, finish this book."*

"I'm sorry."

"You have no need to be, my friend. You have simply played your part, now enjoy the show."

CHAPTER 49

MY CONFESSION

Hi my name is Travis and I'm an insomniac with apeirophobia.

I've felt deja vu on a daily basis since I was a child. Whether I'm brushing my teeth or looking down and noticing the cracks in the sidewalk passing by underfoot, as soon as the feeling overcomes me, my heart starts to race. At first I found it exciting. I wondered if there was some hidden talent that I possessed but was yet unable to hone... Or maybe it was hereditary. One day a great grandparent would approach me with the inevitable speech about great responsibility and our secret Native

American ancestry... My brain always finds the most outlandish and impossible explanations. It's in my nature. I've always had a wild imagination.

Precognition may not be a viable theory, but it was for a long time the most entertaining. Whenever the feeling of deja vu struck me, I would imagine the moment in time as a request for assistance by the forces of fate. My brain was being triggered for a greater good, making me notice something small in that instance and giving me the opportunity to change my path or make a difference in the lives of the less fortunate. I'd roll the dice and turn up four sixes and a two in the middle of a game of Yahtzee and get the feeling of deja vu... instead of re-rolling the two and going for a signature "Yahtzee!", I'd scoop up the sixes and re-roll the four-of-a-kind for more twos. I'd smile and block out the catcalls from my competitors letting me know how stupid I was because deep down inside I knew that with that shake and toss of those four dice, came a change in our timeline and the path of the world around me. I was saving a life or righting a wrong.

Chaos theory and the Butterfly effect became obsessions as a result of my fascination with déjà vu. I began to wonder what good I was doing by each and every action. I began to worry what wrong I was causing with them as well. The worry started to affect my ability to make quick and intelligent decisions. Double and triple guessing each action and choice to see if a double negative would somehow correct the possibility of a mudslide in Rio de Janeiro or a piano falling on a woman pushing her baby in a buggy in Paris...

Time travel fascinated me. From H.G. Wells to Carl Sagan, I wanted to know everything about it. Wormholes, black holes, Einstein's Theory of Relativity, the space-time continuum... I ventured into every aspect of its possibilities. I even went as far as creating markers in time for future time travelers to be able to use as calibration points for their eventual time traveling devices. I waited and wondered. I knew that one day, when I stood in the street looking up at the sky with my sign clearly marking the time and date down to the second that a traveler from the future would magically appear before me with a thank you and a pat on the head. When that moment never arrived, I began to speculate about what that meant. Time was a construct created as a crutch to put boundaries on the things our young minds were unable to comprehend. Time was irrelevant. If time was irrelevant, what else had no point or meaning? Religion? Life? Death? Why are we here? Where is here? What is the meaning of life?

If I'm not worrying about decisions or consequences, I'm questioning the validity of the actions and reactions. Accepting the truths of others leaves no room for the possibility of enlightenment that comes from an answer for which the question was never asked. I ask a lot of questions. It's my nature. I've always had a wild imagination.

What is déjà vu? What does it mean to you?

I have a confession to make. Everything I've done in my life has been leading up to the previous summation of events. One of you just read this. It is going to redefine everything you thought you knew about yourself, about life, about existence.. about *everything*. If you read this book and felt an overwhelming sense of déjà vu, as if you've read it before, maybe you have. You may have related to many of the situations. One of you just read this and it is going to destroy your life.

There is a memory locked deep in my subconscious that's been sitting dormant since I was a child. With the help of The Shadow Man and my own inner voice, the memory fought to reach the surface. For decades I have misconstrued the suppression as just another exaggerated conspiracy created in the wake of my insomnia and apeirophobia, but as the mysteries of my past unraveled so did the answers to the questions that had plagued me across time and space.

When I was a kid, the fear of infinity and the vast nothingness of our existence within the universe drove my parents to send me to countless psychiatrists. All attempted the same thing, but none were able to give me anything more than tools to better accomplish suppressing the fear rather than facing it.

My year spent with Dr Schicksal wasn't a year spent trying to face or even fix my fear; it was a year programming me for this moment. One of you is reading this right now... changing history... *again.*

My fear of infinity is justified. This I now know. That's the only comfort I am finding at the moment.

My last session with Dr Schicksal was the moment when the good doctor explained what had been going on for the last year of my life. I was chosen because of my susceptibility for suggestion and intelligence in conveying a message. A message had been planted in my brain. I was going to eventually find a voice and hand deliver this message to my audience, setting forth a serious of events that would repeat again and again. In fact, these series of events have been repeating for eons. There are no means of stopping the course of time. It must go on.

Everything I've said and done has been leading up to this single moment. The moment where I explain that the one person this book is created for will come back to my childhood and plant this novel. The one person this book is created for will wish the world stranded within a Mobius Strip across time and space. The one person this book is created for will see the world reset itself whenever I'm prompted to share my confession.

The person this book was intended for is going to be in a car crash. The person this book is intended for will suffer a traumatic brain injury. This damage will change the way you see the world, redefining everything. Soon after, you'll attempt to take your own life.

You will fail.

Eventually you'll be back in my childhood, trapped in your past, directing the sessions of hypnosis, prompting this confession, creating the loop in time through my words under the disguise of a professional named after destiny itself. My fear of infinity is justified. This I now know. That's the only comfort I am finding at the moment.

One of you has just read this. You may have read it a thousand times before. One of you has just read this and set into motion a series of events that will change everything. This book just destroyed your life. This book was meant for you.

By reading this, the continuum has come full circle.

I am plagued with new questions now. "Which came first? The book or the doctor? Did he go mad and create the book or did the book drive him to insanity? This is all I can think about whenever I think of this book. Which came first... the book or the doctor? That's it. Just that. Nothing else. Book? Doctor? Book? Doctor? Can't sleep. Book? Doctor? Can't function. Book? Doctor?

I keep telling myself this was simply a fantasy. I keep telling myself you are not going to die. I keep telling myself it's all fiction.

I keep telling myself this is not a confession.

"Someone will read this."

I keep telling myself this is not a confession.

"You will read this."

I keep telling myself this is not a confession.

"I think, therefore I am."

...

Forgive me.

Made in the USA
Charleston, SC
15 April 2012